THE SIGHT OF BLOOD

THE SIGHT OF BLOOD

▼

Michele Taylor

Writers Club Press
San Jose New York Lincoln Shanghai

The Sight of Blood

Writers Club Press
an imprint of iUniverse.com, Inc.

For information address:
iUniverse.com, Inc.
5220 S 16th, Ste. 200
Lincoln, NE 68512
www.iuniverse.com

ISBN: 0-595-18175-9

Printed in the United States of America

For My Aunt Ruth,
who believed.

EPIGRAPH

When Alfred Hitchcock was asked what he thought was the most horrifying thing in the world, the director replied: "Murder by a babbling brook."

CHAPTER ONE

Jerry Tucker slowed his semi down as he approached the bend in the road. This rural one wasn't the usual route truckers took on their runs from Detroit to Chicago. But autumn had come to this part of Michigan in its full glory and the beauty of this stretch from Dowagiac to Summerville in Cass County made Jerry detour off the expressway and drive forty miles out of his way to experience it.

Late October had changed the maples, oaks and birches along each side of the road to every shade of red and gold, yellow and orange, brown and rust. A brisk breeze swayed them gently to and fro. The early morning sun shone down and ignited the leaves' colors to an almost blinding brightness. The sky was a clear, vivid blue and lazy, fluffy, cotton-like clouds drifted across it. It was also Indian Summer, so the cool of the previous days was gone, and gentle warmth had replaced it.

Sitting in the driver's seat of his semi's cab, Jerry took this all in from this high prospective. Tall and burly, with large, thick hands that clasped the steering wheel firmly, Jerry looked every inch the strong, tough trucker. He had longish, light brown hair that was somewhat disheveled and wore a rolled up bandana as a hand around his head. The blue bandana with the white dots contrasted with the yellow plaid flannel shirt he wore under a navy blue down vest. His jeans were faded and his heavy boots were worn. But deep inside Jerry had a kind and tender heart, which was touched now by the beauty of the landscape around him and the promise that this was going to be a gorgeous autumn day.

He passed a sign announcing his entrance into the city limits of the small town of Grangeville, Michigan. Tucked into the southwestern corner of the state, not far from the Indiana border, Grangeville was wrapped around by the Dowagiac River like a protective, loving, and isolating arm. The life of Grangeville centered on Main Street, a main street where well-kept small buildings lined each clean side of it. The population of three thousand people was very friendly and very caring, provided you followed their ways and believed what they believed and acted like they thought you should act. The lifestyle and attitude of the townspeople was as rock solid conservative now, in 1972, as it was when the town was founded in 1868 by a fundamentalist preacher and his obedient flock. However, even Grangeville was not unaffected by the social changes the 1960's sent roaring across the country. Jane Fleming was the prime example of that.

Jerry slowed his truck further as he came out of the bend in the road and approached Pops Griffiths' general store. Homer "Pops" Griffiths' small store was about a mile from the edge of Grangeville, isolated, tucked cozily amidst the forest surrounding Grangeville. It was still very much the old-style general store of many years ago; Pops still had a pickle barrel one could purchase a spear from. It was a definite stop on Jerry's haul when he took his autumn sojourn in Grangeville. Pops Griffiths was the kindliest, friendliest, most beloved old man in Grangeville, and to many, in the whole county. He always had time to chat with his customers, while sharing a cup of hot coffee he always had freshly brewed and available or a candy bar or one of his homemade sandwiches with them. His was not so much a store as a haven for those who found the world had turned too liberal, a place that was a throwback to an earlier, simpler, more traditional time when people *really* cared about each other and everyone knew their place and no one dared stray from the expected behavior of their gender and social order. Pops personified these qualities, and everyone in Grangeville loved Pops. Except for one notable exception.

Jerry applied the brakes and parked his big rig opposite Pops' store. He jumped from the cab and, after glancing up and down the road, ran across.

He bounced up the stairs to the porch, humming merrily to himself, practically tasting Pops' delicious, freshly brewed coffee already. He reached for the screen door and grabbed the handle and pulled.

But nothing happened. The door did not open. Caught by surprise, Jerry stood motionless for a second. Then he tried it again, but the door was obviously still hooked on the inside. Jerry glanced at his watch. Yes, it was past Pops' opening time.

"Pops?" Jerry knocked on the door and attempted to peer in through the screen and front doors. There was no answer and he could see nothing. He also noticed he didn't smell the strong coffee he usually always could from even out here. He knocked again but there was still no answer and Jerry glanced around swiftly. It was then he realized the blinds on the two front windows of the store had not been raised either.

With the small speed but different attitude, Jerry hopped down the steps and headed around the store to the back. He turned the corner to the backyard. The changed trees there in the back rustled slightly as another gentle breeze caressed through their leaves, several of them standing guard along the small pathway that led down to the Dowagiac River where Pops often went fishing. Jerry could hear the faint sound of the Dowagiac rushing by in the distance. Something slowed his pace suddenly, and he realized it was the silence that was so heavy that he could hear the Dowagiac flowing by. A hollow, chilling feeling came over him. But he still walked forward to the back door.

He curled his fingers around the handle and this screen door opened. He tried the back door and it too opened. He walked in.

This was the part of the store Pops lived in, and Jerry stepped into the living room.

"Pops," he called out again, "Pops, it's me. Jerry. Jerry Tucker." He waited a moment for a reply. There was nothing. Now Jerry found the atmosphere in the store very eerie.

He looked around the living room, then through the chintz curtain doorway into the store. Nothing was amiss there. He backtracked into the living quarters.

He looked into the kitchen, which was off the living room. A few clean dishes sat in the drainer by the sink. Jerry left the kitchen and went up the hallway off the living room and opposite the kitchen. The next room was a bedroom. The bed was missing the spread. The blankets and pillows were still there though, and still in place.

Jerry stood a moment in the bedroom doorway like a statue. There was only one more place to look now. The bathroom. Jerry turned his head slowly at first, then his body, towards the room down at the end of the hallway. The door was opened a crack.

Laboriously he stepped towards it, his breath also coming in heavy gasps. He came to the door and his right foot slid a little. He looked down and saw where his boot had slid there was a thin film of red liquid. Jerry did a panicked intake of breath and pushed open the bathroom door.

There, on the floor and leaning up against the bathtub he saw Pops Griffiths, with his mouth open and his eyes staring unseeing right at Jerry. A knife was stuck in the middle of his chest. Bright red and dark blood was everywhere, covering everything: the floor, the wall, the toilet, and Pops.

A noise like a trapped, terrified animal emitted from big Jerry, and he ran through the hallway, living room and out the back door like a maniac, screaming in horror. He ran around the house and blindly towards his truck across the street. A car was coming up just then from town and its driver slammed on the brakes to avoid the screaming Jerry, who fortunately still had enough sense of mind left to dart out of the way.

***

Three Sheriff's cars with their flashers blinking, an ambulance and a forensic team's car were parked in front of and all around Pops' store an hour and a half later. A few civilian cars were parked across the street, with a few curious spectators, mostly young males with nothing else better to do, standing next to them trying to catch a glimpse of anything that might be interesting. All they could see was some strange guy sitting on the porch steps of Pops' store and appearing to be shaking hysterically while a paramedic leaned over him. This proving boring after a short while, a couple of the males tried again to cross the street and get closer, but the two Sheriff's deputies, Clark Alfred and Galen Keyes, standing guard ordered them back again. The spectators moaned and groaned and badmouthed the deputies, though carefully, but returned to their spot across the street.

Sheriff Ralph Parsons supervised it all, from ordering his deputies to keep the spectators back to inspecting the grisly scene of Pops' death. Big, stocky, with a ruddy complexion and reddish hair that was showing more than a few strands of gray and a rapidly developing bloated belly and sagging jowls, fifty-five year old Sheriff Parsons stood in the doorway of the bathroom watching as a photographer continued to take pictures of the crime scene. In all his thirty-odd years in law enforcement this was the bloodiest, most gruesome call he had ever been on. In fact, this was only his second murder case in all that time, the first being a hunting accident that turned out to be no hunting accident at all, but a lover in cahoots with another man's wife to bump off her husband. The dead man had had a big hole in his chest but since everyone had thought it had been only an accident, at first, it didn't seem that ugly. Only after the murder plot had been revealed did Ralph remember the scene as gory, but time had faded the image. This was right before him and definitely no accident.

Behind him Ralph heard the forensic team moving about dusting for fingerprints and examining the rooms for other clues.

"Are you almost done Fred?" Ralph asked the photographer in front of him.

"Not quite Ralph," replied Fred Parker, clicking away nonchalantly. Fred had been a crime scene photographer in Detroit and Chicago and this was nothing new to him, so he was completely unaffected by the scene before him. Ralph sighed uncomfortably while looking at the scene, while not really looking at the scene.

Outside, unordered by Ralph, another Sheriff's car pulled up and parked in front of Pops' store. Its appearance caused a slight buzz in the bored spectators till its driver emerged, and that caused the buzz to get louder. The driver was Grangeville Deputy Sheriff Jane Fleming.

Some of the young males yelled out some derogatory remarks to Jane regarding her sex and her job and her sex and job together as she started walking towards the front of Pops' store. She ignored the remarks and those who made them. Also she ignored the resentful glances of her fellow deputies Clark and Galen standing guard and of the paramedics attempting to calm the still unnerved Jerry. She went up to Clark and nodded once in the direction of Jerry.

"That who found Pops?" she asked Clark.

Tall, gangly, black-haired Clark looked at Jane with barely concealed dislike in his blue eyes.

"Yeah," he said in almost a snarl.

"What's his name?" asked Jane, ignoring Clark's attitude.

"Don't know," said Clark.

"Can't he talk?" asked Jane, looking up at Clark.

"Haven't been able to get a word out of him. Driver who almost ran him over when he came running out of the store is the one who called us."

Jane looked at the man again and started walking towards him. Clark scowled after her, wondering what she could do that he and Galen and all the male paramedics hadn't done already.

Jane came up to the porch where the paramedics were still trying to calm Jerry. He sat on the top step of the porch, still shaking and swallowing hard. The paramedic next to Jerry suddenly produced a hypodermic needle from his kit when Jane tapped him on the arm.

"Mind if I try speaking to him a minute before you try that?" she asked quietly and calmly.

The paramedic looked skeptical and annoyed at Jane, but stepped aside. Jane sat on the step next to Jerry.

"I'm Deputy Sheriff Jane Fleming," she said to him, "May I see your driver's license please?" she asked.

Clark, Galen and the paramedics all gritted their teeth in disgust at themselves for not thinking of that themselves, and in resentment of Jane for thinking it. As they watched and to their mounting annoyance Jerry reached into his back pocket and brought out a wallet. With shaking fingers he handed it to Jane.

"Please take it out of the wallet for me," said Jane quietly and businesslike.

With continued shaking fingers, Jerry managed to get the license out after about a minute, which Jane waited through patiently.

"Thank you," she said, taking it from Jerry's now slightly less shaking fingers.

"You are Gerald Norman Tucker, from Detroit?" asked Jane, as she read the license. Jerry managed one nod in response.

"Is that your rig over there?" Jane asked, indicating the semi still parked across the street.

Jerry now managed two nods to Jane's questions. Though Jane's manner was cool and collective, there was sympathy and understanding in her eyes and voice where there had been none in the deputies' or the paramedics'. Here was finally someone who guessed that what he had seen in the back of Pops' store had almost driven him out of his mind. Her next words proved that.

"I know it had to have been terrifying for you to find Pops Griffiths like this Jerry. May I call you Jerry?"

"Yes," Jerry got out clearly, sending surprised looks between the paramedics and deputies at the first coherent word out of Jerry's mouth. They began watching and listening to Jane's questioning in earnest in spite of themselves and their annoyance at her.

"What are you hauling over there?" asked Jane, indicating the semi again with a nod of her head.

"Transmission parts."

"Where are you heading?"

"Chicago."

"You're a little out of your way if you were heading to Chicago from Detroit. How come?" asked Jane.

"I drove out to come through here. I…I think it's nice around here, in the Fall. It's…pretty," stammered Jerry.

"You stop and see Pops too?"

"Yeah. But I wish I hadn't now," said Jerry, shaking his head.

"I know," said Jane.

Despite the reawakened memory of discovering Pops, Jerry did not lose control and start to shake again. Jane was so sympathetic and so calm herself that she was a steadying influence on him. He swallowed hard one last time.

"Jerry, will you tell me how you came to find Pops?" Jane asked.

Slowly, but now calmly, and to the astonishment of the other deputies and paramedics, Jerry related his story. Jane watched him carefully, which made it easier for him to talk.

"Jerry, is there anything you can tell us that might help us find out who did this to Pops?" asked Jane, when Jerry finished.

Jerry shook his head calmly.

"No. I didn't see anything."

"I believe you," said Jane, and, to the further surprise of the men surrounding him, Jerry managed a small smile.

"But if you remember anything later, you let us know, all right?" Jane added.

"I will. Can I…can I go now? I gotta be in Chicago by three," said Jerry.

"Sure. But, how about a cup of coffee first? Clark, would you go in my patrol car and get my thermos? I think I have about a cup left in it."

Clark narrowed his eyes at what he perceived as an order from Jane and not just a request.

"Get it yourself," he snapped.

Both Jane and Jerry looked up at him, Jane's expression going blank but Jerry openly angry towards Clark. Jane stood.

"All right."

She walked down the steps and back to her patrol car and brought out the tall thermos from the front seat. But before she could start back, a civilian's car pulled up behind her patrol car and parked. Pausing, recognizing the car, Jane waited as the driver got out. He was already smiling at Jane even before he emerged. It was the owner, editor and chief reporter of the Grangeville Chronicle, Timothy Usher.

Even though Jane was already in an involved relationship, she did not fail to notice that Timothy Usher had to be one of the best-looking men walking the face of the earth, if not ever walked the face of the earth. He had a mannequin-perfection to his looks, clean-cut curves and lines made up the features of his face. He had dark brown hair that was semi-long in length and rakishly parted on the side, failing onto his forehead and partially covering his thick left eyebrow that almost joined the right in the middle of his brow above his nose. He had hazel eyes and that darkening in his complexion where his whiskers grew on his face, which Jane had always found sexy in a man. He was tall, over six feet, and was just muscular enough.

Tim, like Jane, was originally from Detroit. In the sixties he had been one of those radical student journalists in college and afterwards with a radical newspaper. But with the advent of the seventies came his thirtieth birthday, and when he heard the small Grangeville Chronicle was for sale, he bought it last July from old Mr. Anderson, who was retiring. When asked why, after his firebrand background, he ended up buying a small town newspaper to run and report on the rather mundane happenings there, Tim replied: "I reached thirty. I couldn't trust myself anymore."

But one of the first things he did when he assumed ownership of the Chronicle was to come out in favor of Jane Fleming being in the Sheriff's Department with a fiery editorial. Jane had just joined the department the April before, yet she was still the talk of the town and bitterly resented by practically everyone. Tim paid a visit to the Sheriff's Department to meet Jane when he got word of this situation of a lady cop on the force. From the moment he saw her, he was more than just automatically behind her in her struggle to be accepted as a cop. Tim Usher was totally smitten with Jane Fleming. But he had heard too, of her, that she had become involved with someone else in town, which, because of the extent of that relationship, also made her the talk of the town and the object of anger amongst the townspeople. So as much as he would have liked to otherwise, Tim granted that Jane was another man's woman, and became only friends with her. They had a good working relationship too, Jane becoming Tim's connection to the Grangeville Sheriff's Department. But Tim did not write off ever becoming more than a friend to Jane and she his link to the Sheriff's Department if this thing she had with that Przybylski fellow ever petered out.

Jane smiled, too, when she saw Tim. Her relationship with Butch was strong enough to allow her to like Tim Usher as a friend and confidant regarding department business with no misgivings or trouble from Butch. But unlike Tim, Jane never imagined their relationship farther than friend and confidant. Butch was everything to her, and it never dawned on Jane Tim could be more, or would like to be more if the situation rose. If she suspected in the back of her mind Tim was actually in love with her, Jane did not realize it.

"We got an actual murder here, Deputy?" asked Tim, coming around the patrol car to stand before Jane. It looked like Tim had dressed in a hurry. His worn jeans, T-shirt, tennis shoes and down jacket looked like they had been thrown on.

"How did you hear about it?" asked Jane.

"I caught the report on my police band radio this morning just as I was getting up," said Tim.

"You monitor the police band?" asked Jane.

"A habit. From years ago," said Tim, as he grinned. "So what's the story with Pops Griffiths?" he asked, following Jane as she started back to the store with the thermos.

"I don't know. I haven't been to the crime scene yet," said Jane.

"Anything on the O'Brien case?" asked Tim. Jane shook her head no.

Tim fell back behind Jane as she approached the stairs and Jerry Tucker. Tim brought out a notepad and pen as Jane poured a grateful and now obviously on her side Jerry the last of the black coffee into the cup, which was the thermos lid.

"How is it?" she asked, as Jerry took a swallow.

"Fine," said Jerry, eyeing Clark just as angrily as Clark had looked at Jane a moment before. Then his glance went to Tim standing in front of him.

"Who are you?" Jerry asked.

"Tim Usher. Owner, and reporter for the Grangeville Chronicle," he replied.

"Usher, why don't you get the hell out of here?" said Clark.

Clark didn't care for Tim since Tim's editorial in favor of Jane, and treated Tim with even more disdain than he treated Jane. But not too much more. Tim was a tall man, a good several inches taller than Clark.

"I'm doing my job, Deputy, as you're doing yours," said Tim, unconcerned with Clark or his attitude. He looked back at Jerry. "Who are you?"

"Jerry Tucker," he replied.

"He's a truck driver from Detroit. He discovered Pops' body," said Jane.

Tim busily wrote this down. "Mind answering a few questions Mr. Tucker?" asked Tim, when he finished.

Jerry glanced at Jane, as if to see what she thought he should do. Jane nodded at Tim.

"Talk to Mr. Usher while you're finishing your coffee," said Jane. Tim and Jerry then went into a question and answer conversation, and Jane started off around the side of the store towards the back.

"Hey, you can't go back there!" snapped Clark after her, "Sheriff said nobody allowed."

"I'm no nobody, Deputy," said Jane, as her parting shot.

The yellow police tape bobbed up and down in the breeze as it cordoned off the back of the store, and Jane stooped to walk under it and approach the door.

She walked down the hallway towards the bathroom in the back. Pausing at the bedroom, Jane glanced in, noticing that the bedspread was missing. Then she walked up next to Ralph who was still standing in the bathroom doorway. Jane looked into the bathroom, expressionless. Ralph glanced at Jane.

Ralph at first had absolutely detested the idea of a woman deputy. But Jane had threatened to take the Sheriff's Department to court if not given the job, a job she had all the credentials for, except maleness. The city council and the mayor were no happier with the idea of a female deputy in the Grangeville Sheriff's Department than Ralph, but they liked less the idea of the court battle she threatened them with. The glare of the spotlight such a suit would place on privacy-loving Grangeville was more reprehensible to the city council and mayor than actually having a female deputy, so reluctantly they gave in. Ralph was even more reluctant, in fact he was downright against it, but he had no choice but to take Jane onto his force. Though he would never admit it out loud, Ralph finally had to admit to himself after a few months Jane was a good law enforcement officer. Grudgingly, he grew to at least tolerate her, but she still was like a burr under a saddle to him whenever he saw her. Plus there was that touch of discomfort he always felt around women. Young, vibrant women like Jane, anyway.

"What are you doing here Deputy?" he asked her, somewhat sharply.

"I heard the call over the radio," said Jane, having no trouble with staring at the crime scene, mesmerized. Then she stepped carefully into the bathroom. Ralph could not bring himself to step in further, and resented Jane's obviously easy entrance into the room. She stepped around the bloody area, looking carefully at every object as the photographer finished up.

"Okay," he said, "I'm done. You can have the coroner take the body when he comes." Fred stepped out, leaving Ralph in the doorway and Jane in the room. She was standing next to the toilet, which was covered with blood and also filled with it, staring down into it. She took a deep breath, and then a conclusive look came over her face, which Ralph, too perturbed at her, didn't notice.

"All right, Deputy. Get out of there," said Ralph briskly.

"Just a minute, Sheriff," said Jane. She stepped carefully to Pops' body and squatted down, looking at it intently. To Ralph's utter surprise and shock she picked up Pops' hand and gently twisted and turned it around.

"I'd say Pops has been dead, oh, roughly eleven hours," said Jane, "That means he was killed about nine o'clock last night," she added, glancing at her watch.

"How can you tell?" asked Ralph, curious in spite of his shock at Jane touching the body.

"By the amount of rigor mortis that's set in," said Jane. She carefully put Pops' hand down while Ralph cringed all over again at the mention of rigor mortis. Jane stood up and turned towards Ralph, her hands resting on her heavy gun belt around her waist.

"What's your theory about this, Sheriff?" asked Jane.

Ralph had been too overcome by the murder to theorize anything yet, but he did not want to admit to Jane he hadn't, so in desperation he blurted out the most common explanation for such a murder as Pops'.

"Robbery."

"Robbery?" said Jane, stunned, "Did you check the cash register?"

"No. Not yet."

"Well, the money's still there. Pops wasn't killed for his money."

Ralph scowled, hating to have her contradict him.

"You mean you don't think this was a robbery."

"I don't think. I know it wasn't a robbery."

"Well then, what was it?" asked Ralph, annoyed. "Someone had to come in to rob Pops' store, Pops caught him, fought with him and Pops was killed."

"In the bathroom, Sheriff?" asked Jane solemnly.

Ralph was taken aback at this piece of realization and looked at Jane, struck speechless. Jane looked around the room again.

"There was a struggle, yes, here, in the bathroom. Pops had to have been in here when he was killed. It's what he was doing in here..." Jane's voice trailed off softly as she seemed to catch herself from saying more.

Ralph, now perturbed at being shown up by Jane regarding this theory, didn't catch the last part of her speculation.

"So why do you think he was killed?" asked Ralph.

Jane looked at Ralph again with a reluctant look on her face.

"Sheriff, if I told you what I thought, you wouldn't believe me. You wouldn't **want** to believe me."

Ralph scowled again at Jane. That was another thing about Jane that aggravated him. She was so much the maverick, the rebel, almost a hot dogger. But it didn't occur to Ralph that the reason for that might have been the hands-off way of dealing with her by himself and the other deputies. She was never really taken into the confidence at the Sheriff's office, they basically worked *around* Jane instead of including her in the work. Ralph and his other deputies did their job together and left Jane to do hers alone. She did not always find that easy to do. Support would have been nice sometime. Fortunately she had Butch for that. But Butch was not on the police force.

The noise of a scuffle was heard in the kitchen and Jane's and Ralph's attention were called to it. A moment later Tim appeared in the doorway next to Ralph. He took one look in the room and his eyes widened.

"Holy shit," he said.

Clark showed up a split second later, and grabbed Tim's arm.

"I'm sorry Sheriff. I tried to keep him out of here but he forced his way," said Clark. He indicated Tim to follow him with a motion of his head. "C'mon buddy. Let's go."

It's…okay, Deputy. He can stay," said Ralph. He didn't care for Tim either, because of Tim' radical past, and his coming out in support of Jane and the harsh criticism of the department that editorial had contained. But while Ralph was unworldly in many ways he knew the power of the press, and had a more than healthy respect for it. Clark let Tim go with a slight scowl.

Tim let out a long, low whistle as he stepped in next to Jane and looked around. His look then stopped at Pops' body and lingered on it. He didn't flinch or cringe.

"It doesn't seem to bother you," Jane whispered to him.

Tim looked at Jane solemnly.

"Deputy, I've seen things that make this look like a Norman Rockwell painting," said Tim.

Galen Keyes walked up then. Short, slim, baby-faced Galen was twenty-four years old, with wavy blonde hair and blue eyes framed by wire-rimmed granny glasses, and if there was anyone who wasn't suited to be a law enforcement officer, it was Galen. He seemed to go into a nervous fit when he had to write a ticket. But as long as things remained orderly and he simply had to stand there and look the deputy, he was fine, and even a little cocky. That was all he had been doing up to now in front of the store; he had not been inside to see the murder scene, so he strode up confidently.

"Coroner is here, Sheriff," he said to Ralph. Then Galen's eyes went into the bathroom, and his face went white. Jane always felt just the tiniest bit amused when the air was let out of Galen's balloon and he looked and acted like the bumbling incompetent he really was, and she felt it now. But this time she felt sympathetic too when she noticed Galen was going to be sick.

"Are you all right Galen?" asked Ralph, noticing only something was wrong with Galen but not realizing what.

"Excuse us Sheriff," said Jane, and walked quickly up to Galen. She grabbed his arm and pulled him stumbling down the hall and outside, where she held his head while he upchucked in the backyard.

"You all right now Deputy?" Jane asked, quite businesslike and unemotionally, when Galen finally raised his head. He nodded a few times and looked at Jane ashamedly, doubly so at vomiting in front of a fellow deputy, plus a woman at that, a woman who was handing the situation with complete professionalism. But it was that professionalism that immediately put his embarrassment to rest.

"It isn't a pretty sight, Deputy," Jane added strongly, yet understandingly. Galen took comfort from her tone and the hand she slapped gently on his shoulder. Galen had never really hated Jane when she came on the force, but treated her shabbily because the other men had. Now though, after this, that wasn't a good enough reason anymore, and he smiled weakly, genuinely, at her, and Jane smiled back.

"You stay out here and get some fresh air. I'll go back in and help the coroner," said Jane.

The coroner, Drew Phillips, and his men had gone in while Jane was attending to Galen, and were on their way out when Jane came back into the store. The two attendants carried the stretcher with the big black bag containing Pops on it outside, causing Galen to almost get sick all over again when he saw it.

"What can you tell us about the death, Doctor'?" Jane asked Phillips, a short, little, gray-haired man. He wore his glasses forever perched on his nose even though they were bifocals. He stopped and looked at Jane over them, critical of her choice of career as well, and also slightly amazed that a woman had not been set off screaming and fainting at the bloody sight of Pops' murder, and it was the male deputy who had lost his cookies over it.

"Can't tell you too much till I perform the autopsy," he said shortly." But I can tell you the victim has been dead for approximately eleven hours."

Ralph, standing behind Phillips, scowled hearing Jane's estimate had been correct. Jane only nodded concurrently. Tim, behind Ralph, wrote it down.

"And it appears he has been stabbed several times by someone who is very strong. The knife appears to have cracked the sternum right in two."

Tim again worked on his notes. Galen, who happened to step inside at the very moment Coroner Phillips described the wounds, went white all over again, and turned back outside, holding his mouth. Again Phillips looked amazed that the female deputy narily blinked an eye.

"How soon before you have a complete report?" asked Ralph.

Phillips sighed, thinking a moment.

"Tuesday. Wednesday at the latest. Anybody know if this man has any family?"

Ralph looked thoughtful for a moment. "I don't know. I don't remember ever hearing Pops mention any family."

"Well, we need to notify the next of kin, if he has any," said Phillips.

"We can go through his belongings and let your know," said Jane.

Ralph again was annoyed at Jane outthinking him. Phillips nodded curtly at Jane, and left.

"I'd better get going too," said Tim, "If I hurry I can get this in today's edition." Ralph scowled a little at this. The Grangeville Chronicle only came out twice a week, Tuesdays and Fridays, and Ralph would have liked it better if this could have been kept out of the paper till next Tuesday, when he might have made some headway into this case with any leads he would get from the coroner's and forensics' reports. Of course it wasn't that the townspeople wouldn't hear about this, those gawkers outside proved that. But Ralph would have like it if the newspaper account would contain a few details that reassured the town that he was close to solving this crime. He almost asked Tim not to rush this in the paper, but decided Tim was not the type of newspaperman to do something like that, at least for him. So Ralph only watched as Tim started to follow Phillips out.

But Tim stopped at the door and motioned to Jane. She went over to him.

"You'll let me know if you find anything in Pops' belongings," Tim whispered to him.

"Of course," said Jane.

She and Tim shared a smile sealing their agreement, and then Tim left. Ralph couldn't hear what they said exactly, he got the impression a deal had been made though. He realized Tim would probably have sat on the story if Jane had asked him to, and again Ralph felt annoyance at Jane for having an advantage over him.

"Would you like me to take the bedroom, Sheriff?" asked Jane, turning from the door. Ralph had been brooding a little about Jane and her question startled him. Then the mention of the word "bedroom" took him aback.

"The bedroom?" he said nervously.

"Would you like me to search Pops' bedroom for his personal records that might lead us to his family," said Jane.

"Oh. Yes. Do that, Deputy," said Ralph, regaining his poise. If Jane noticed his discomfort of a moment before she didn't let on, and only nodded and walked off down the hallway to the bedroom.

Ralph heard her moving about the room searching it, then went past the chintz curtain into the store. He went behind the counter and began to check the shelves and drawers in it. The cash register caught his eye. With trepidation he hit the key, which opened the drawer. The drawer ejected out and Ralph saw it was filled with money, obviously untouched.

"I think we have a relative of Pops' listed in here," said Jane, Ralph's head jerking up to find her standing next to the open cash drawer. She was holding an old address book open to about the middle. "A Sylvia Griffiths. Living in Chicago."

Jane's eyes dropped to the open drawer and all the money still left in it. Ralph's expression became slightly chagrined but Jane's look showed no reaction to her earlier statement being correct. She only looked up again at Ralph.

"I'll go back to the office and call her about Pops. There's a phone number listed here as well."

"I'll do that," said Ralph, taking the book from her somewhat briskly, "I want you to concentrate on the O'Brien case, Deputy."

Ralph expected some argument from Jane, but to his surprise she said nothing. She did look a little perturbed, but that disappeared after a moment.

"Yes Sheriff," she said.

Now Ralph was suspicious at Jane's acquiescence. The O'Brien case was important, the teenage daughter of a local family had failed to come home from a date last night, but this was a murder case, and Ralph knew Jane well enough now that as a dedicated, smart, law enforcement officer she would want to be in on the investigation. So her lack of resistance made him wary of the reason. He decided to try and find out why.

"What did you find out around Pebble Creek?" he asked.

"No sign of the O'Brien girl, Sheriff," said Jane.

"No clues at all regarding her disappearance?"

"No Sheriff. But I would still like to continue with the investigation."

Now Ralph was really suspicious of Jane's motives. But he preferred for her to handle this case than the murder, and nodded in agreement.

"Very well. But, you are scheduled to go off-duty for the weekend in about an hour." Ralph glanced at his watch. "Turn over the file and your notes to Galen, and let him continue the investigation."

"*Galen*, Sheriff?" said Jane, incredulously.

"Yes, Galen," said Ralph. He saw Jane rolled her eyes slightly as they walked out of the store and back outside. The coroner's hearse was just pulling out and the ambulance was gone, as well as the forensic team's car. Tim's car was seen pulling away. Jerry Tucker was standing up now chatting with Clark as if nothing had come over him. Jane walked over to them and picked up her thermos. As she screwed the cap and cup onto it she looked at Jerry and smiled. But Jerry returned the smile with a look of contempt, sharing the look with Clark a moment. Jane's smile disappeared and she returned Jerry's look with a blank one.

"You're welcome for the coffee," she said flatly, put the thermos under her arm and walked off stately.

Jane got into her patrol car and sat for a moment before starting it. Ralph drove towards hers and saw her in deep thought. His curiosity still nagged at him as to why Jane agreed so easily to remain on the O'Brien case, and made him try again to find out. He stopped his patrol car next to hers, driver's side to driver's side, and rolled down his window. This caught Jane's attention and she rolled down her window too.

"Something on your mind, Deputy?" he asked.

"I was just thinking, Sheriff," said Jane, a touch too lightheartedly.

"About what?" pressed Ralph.

Jane paused a second before replying. She didn't want to tell Ralph this, for she knew his reaction would be unpleasant at best, outraged at the worst. But he obviously was not going to be just shaken off.

"About how these two things happened right after each other: Jennie O'Brien's disappearance and Pops Griffiths' murder," she said.

"And you think there's some kind of *connection?*" said Ralph, stunned. So here was why Jane had not balked at being ordered to remain on the O'Brien case. Ralph slowly shook his head as he regained his composure. "Well, forget it. There is no connection. There can't possibly be."

Ralph took off in his patrol car, leaving his only female deputy to watch him leave. But you're wrong, Sheriff, she was now thinking as she saw in her car. There *could* possibly be a connection between Pops' murder and the O'Brien girl's disappearance. Jane found the evidence for it in the blood-washed bathroom murder scene. But she could not tell her theory of the connection to anyone, except Butch, because it suggested something that just didn't happen in a place like Grangeville.

CHAPTER TWO

Last night was the first time in the months that Jane won her place in the Grangeville Sheriff's Department that Ralph was glad, at least for a few hours, she was part of it. He was glad he had a woman along with him as he drove up to Dolores and Bill O'Brien's house on Yarmouth Street, in the residential part of town.

The call came in at midnight, just after Jane and Clark arrived at the Sheriff's office for the graveyard shift along with the other deputies assigned to it. The building that the Grangeville Sheriff's Department was in was a large, imposing structure of tan brick situated almost in the middle of town. It was reflective of the importance the town put on law and order. There were holding cells in the back of the building, a wide reception area in front and in between them the space where the deputies worked, with several desks, one in particular each deputy eventually gravitated to when they joined the force to write their reports. Jane started using one Clark and another deputy regularly used, but soon found they stopped when they noticed she did too, and she then had it all to herself. Which she didn't mind at all, except it was another example of her outsider status with the department. Ralph had his own office, a room off the deputies' area, and his name and title painted on the frosted glass panel of the door. He was coming out of it now to go home, his shift ending. Just as he passed the reception area the phone rang, and he answered it.

"Grangeville Sheriff's Department," he said. There was a pause as Ralph scowled. "What? Who is this?"

Ralph's words and expression stopped Jane's and Clark's movement and they stood watching and listening to him. As Ralph listened his expression became one of concern. "Dolores. Calm down. Take it easy. Yes, I'll be right over." Ralph hung up the phone and looked at Jane and Clark, the two deputies standing closest to him. It was at this moment he was glad one of them was a female.

"That was Dolores O'Brien," he said, "Their daughter Jennie has not returned home from her date."

"I'll go with you Sheriff," said Clark, slipping his jacket back on.

"Err…no, Clark," said Ralph. And Clark looked startled. "Jane…better come with me."

Jane did not look surprised but simply nodded and put her brown jacket back on. Clark, open mouthed and stunned, watched them leave.

Jane followed Ralph in her own patrol car and parked behind his on the street in front of the O'Brien's white house. All the houses here were meticulously kept up and the yards were neatly groomed, hardly the area where you would expect anything wrong to happen much worse than the lighter fluid not working on the charcoal in the barbeque grill. The porch light was on. Ralph got out and waited for Jane to come up next to him before starting up the walkway. This was a foreign situation for him, dealing with the frantic and terrified mother of a missing child. Things like this never happened in Grangeville, decent children just did not disappear. This called for the sympathies and the empathy of a woman, and although Ralph wasn't sure just how much of these qualities Jane possessed, he knew however much she did, it was more than he, a man and a confirmed bachelor, had.

He walked up the sidewalk with Jane right behind him to his left, and they mounted the whitewashed porch steps towards the front door. The porch was clear of any plants and furniture, in preparation for the coming winter months. Ralph rang the doorbell and waited. There was the sound of footsteps approaching the door from inside and a moment later the wooden door opened. Bill O'Brien stood behind the storm door looking out at them. He looked haggard and sick.

"Ralph," he said, his voice heavy with worry and weariness. His eyes caught sight of Jane and for a split second a look of distrust and dislike crossed his face. But worry came flooding back and he opened the screen door for both Ralph and Jane. They entered into the living room.

Dolores O'Brien sat on the sofa, her hair slightly straggling in her face and her eyes red from crying. She clutched a soggy handkerchief in her hands which she nervously pulled at between dabbing at her eyes. Next to her sat the O'Brien's fourteen year old son Charlie, who was attempting to comfort his mother.

William O'Brien was forty-five, tall, thin, with black hair rapidly being replaced with white, not gray. His clothes seem to hang on him, no matter if he wore a suit, or a shirt and jeans, as he was wearing now.

His wife Dolores, forty-three, was pretty and on the plump side. In contrast to her husband, her thick dark hair had no touch of gray in it. Both she and her husband were native to Grangeville, where Bill owned and ran the town's hardware store, which he inherited from his father.

Their son, Charles, resembled his father. Tall, but not so gaunt, he had black hair that hung somewhat shaggily around his eyes. He wore the worried look also on his parent's faces but along with worry was a look of confusion, not knowing what exactly to say and do in this situation. There was also the smallest touch of guilt in his look, which the other men didn't notice and Dolores was too upset to see. But Jane spotted it right away.

Ralph also felt confused but kept himself from showing it. If he didn't know exactly how to handle this, he could at least look as if he was in charge of the situation.

He and Jane took off their hats. Dolores and Charlie looked up, Charlie somewhat scowled at the sight of Jane but Dolores, too overcome with fright and worry, did not react to Jane adversely.

"Bill. Dolores. Charlie." Ralph acknowledged each of the O'Briens. Jane waited for him to introduce her but he said nothing. So Jane pursed her lips together a moment to control her annoyance, then introduced herself.

"Oh Ralph! You just have to find Jennie! I've been going out of my mind!" wailed Dolores, as a fresh wave of tears came pouring out of her eyes, "She's never done anything like this before, not come home!"

"We'll find her, Dolores," said Ralph limply, uncomfortably.

"Please. Sit down," said Bill.

"Thanks," said Ralph; gratefully, he had still something to keep his lack of idea of what to do next from becoming evident. He sat on a nearby armchair while Bill O'Brien went and sat on the other side of his wife. But Jane remained standing. Stoically she walked to the fireplace and stood, glancing at the mantel. Several portraits in frames lined it, portraits of the O'Brien family members including one that must have been Jennie. She was a typically beautiful small-town teenage girl, with golden brown hair which was long and framed her head and face and brown eyes. Next to her portrait was a photo of Jennie posing with a handsome, blond, tall young man, both dressed for a prom.

Jane looked at Ralph expectantly, but Ralph simply sat there and adjusted his holster. All three O'Briens looked at him, waiting too. Jane saw him swallow hard and realizing then Ralph had no idea what to do, she pulled out her pen and notepad from her breast pocket.

"How old is your daughter, Mr. and Mrs. O'Brien?" she asked calmly.

Bill O'Brien looked annoyed and relieved at the same time at Jane; relieved official action was now being taken regarding his daughter's disappearance, but annoyed it was with this woman deputy. Bill remained silent but Dolores, in her state of mind, had no qualms answering Jane.

"Sixteen," she said, and Jane made a note of her reply.

"When was the last time you saw your daughter?"

"Seven o'clock."

"Was that here at home?" Jane asked.

"Yes. Here. At home. Steve picked her up for a date. They were going to the movies," said Dolores.

"Steve?"

"Steve Ballard."

"Is he her boyfriend?" asked Jane.

"Yes," said Bill, finally deciding the woman deputy rated saying something to her questions.

Jane wrote his name down.

"Have you talked to him about Jennie not showing up home?" asked Jane.

"Yes. Bill just got off the phone with him. He said they went to the movies, and then..." Dolores looked a little embarrassed through her worry, "...went up to Pebble Creek."

"I see," said Jane, writing it down.

Pebble Creek was a branch of the Dowagiac River whose surrounding acres had been made into a city park and recreation area. It was hilly in some places and Grangeville could be seen below from many of the hills, and couples parked there on the hills at night, though none of them spent much time enjoying the view of Grangeville's lights. Jane knew this because she and Butch went up there often but for the life of her she couldn't remember what the view looked like.

"And did Steve tell you what happened up there?" asked Jane.

"He said they got into an argument. Jennie got mad and ran off," said Bill.

"Did he try and follow her?" asked Jane.

"He didn't say," said Bill.

"What was the argument about?"

"He didn't say, either," said Bill.

Jane flipped her notepad shut. "I think we should go have a talk with this young man, Sheriff," she said.

Ralph reacted somewhat in surprise at the sudden attention to him. He had listened while Jane questioned the O'Briens, resentment stirring in him a little at Jane for knowing what to do, yet fascinated at her professionalism and the way she was getting the exact information they needed. He quickly regained his poise and stood, nodding.

"You don't think Steve has anything to do with this?" said Bill.

"This is what we'll find out when we talk to him," said Jane.

Ralph put his hat on and stepped to leave. But Jane turned to the mantel behind her again.

"Mrs. O'Brien, may I have this picture of your daughter for the APB?" Jane asked gently but firmly.

"For the what?" asked Dolores, sniffling but curious.

"All Points Bulletin. We send a report to all law-enforcement depart-ments in the county notifying them we are looking for a missing person. It helps to have a picture of them."

"Oh," said Dolores. She stood and went to the mantel and carefully took the portrait down and out of the frame. Lovingly she looked at the photo, then handed it to Jane.

"You will give it back?" she asked.

"Of course."

"Thank you," she whispered, and nodded.

Charlie O'Brien got up and put a comforting arm around his mother as she inhaled with a shudder and covered her eyes with her handkerchief. Jane eyed him again, and again she saw the touch of guilt in the fourteen year old's face. That teenager knew something, and Jane wished she could talk to him alone right now, but to request so would no doubt draw resist-ance and questions from everyone and Jane was not ready to explain her demand. She put her hat on too.

"Take care now," said Ralph, as he and Jane left the house, "We'll do our best to find Jennie and bring her back safe and sound."

Bill O'Brien shut the door behind Jane and Ralph as they stepped out of the house and onto the porch.

"Get back to the office and get that APB out on Jennie O'Brien right away," said Ralph was they walked down the sidewalk towards their cars, "I'll go to the Ballard residence and question Steve Ballard." Questioning a young man about his night's activities was more in line with what Ralph felt he could handle, so he didn't need Jane anymore and felt comfortable ordering her off on another duty. But Jane resisted.

"I'll radio it in and have Clark at least get the information out," said Jane, "I'd like to be there when you question the Ballard boy, Sheriff."

"Why?" Ralph asked, stopping at his car and looking at Jane puzzled.

"I would like to hear his account of tonight too."

"You can read my report."

"I would like to be there to see him too during the questioning."

Her tone was tinged with a steely touch of annoyance but Ralph easily dismissed that. What he couldn't dismiss so easily, actually not at all, was the eyeball to eyeball look she was giving him, filled with the same determination she had when she told Ralph she was filing suit in court to get on the force. Ralph wavered under that look of a strong woman back then and wavered under it now. Slightly intimidated, he gave in.

"Very well Deputy. Radio in the APB and follow me to the Ballard home."

"Yes Sheriff," said Jane matter-of-factly, as if she had met no resistance.

As Jane walked back to her patrol car it struck Ralph then as odd that Jane wanted to *see* this Ballard boy during the questioning. But not coming up with any rational explanation, he shrugged the thought off and started his car.

The Ballard house was lit inside as Jane and Ralph pulled up. Just a few streets over from the O'Brien house, it too was neatly painted and maintained. Again Jane and Ralph walked up to the porch and Ralph again ran the doorbell. A moment later the porch light came on and the front door opened.

"Sheriff. We knew you'd be stopping by. Come in."

"Thank you Jack," said Ralph.

Jack Ballard stepped back as Ralph opened the screen door and walked in, and the same look of distrust and dislike that appeared on Bill O'Brien's face appeared on Jack Ballard's, only there was no great worry to wash it away and he continued to look at Jane that way. She ignored it as she followed Ralph in, removing her hat.

Mrs. Ballard was sitting on the sofa in a bathrobe next to a tall young man Jane recognized from the prom portrait with Jennie. Steve was husky, a powerfully built young man for only seventeen years old. Jane had thought this from the picture of Jennie and him on the O'Briens' mantel, and it was reinforced at seeing him in person. Though right now, he also looked sleepy and distracted, as he sat next to his mother in his pajamas and robe and obviously, at least to Jane, that he much rather be in bed right now than sitting up with all these people.

Ralph greeted Mrs. Ballard cordially and she returned the sentiment. But when she saw Jane the cordiality flew out of her expression swiftly. Mrs. Arlene Ballard did not restrain her thoughts about Jane as her husband and Bill O'Brien had, and she spoke them right out.

"Young woman, you have no right being a Sheriff's deputy and I don't like you here in my home!" she stated firmly.

Ralph's look dropped embarrassingly but Jane, in an effort that would have made Butch proud, kept her head and her dignity and looked at Mrs. Ballard unflinchingly.

"But I am a duly-sworn Sheriff's deputy, Mrs. Ballard, and I need to be in your home to do my job. Now you have the right to request that I leave here and I shall leave if you do. But I hope our mutual goal of finding out what happened to Jennie O'Brien will permit you to allow me to stay," said Jane.

A small flash of admiration crossed Arlene's face but disappeared immediately. Her expression became solemn and she nodded. Ralph looked at his deputy briefly with admiration too, but it swiftly vanished from his face when he turned his attention back to Steve, who was yawning as he sat on the sofa.

"Steve, would you tell us what happened while you and Jennie were up in Pebble Creek?" Ralph asked him.

Jane took out her pen and notepad again and prepared to take notes. She waited as did the others for Steve to speak, but he just sat there staring sleepily in front of himself.

"You know she's missing, don't you Steve? She hasn't come home. The O'Briens said you told them the two of you had an argument, and Jennie ran off. Is that right?" asked Ralph.

"Yeah. That's what happened," said Steve flatly.

Jane watched Steve closely and found it odd he wasn't more concerned his girlfriend hadn't come home. But she was the only one to think so, for Ralph only looked pleased that the information they had was correct, and the Ballards were obviously too doting on their son to imagine anything he'd say or do was ever unusual.

"Would you tell us what the argument was about?" asked Jane."

Steve looked up and finally some strong emotion appeared on his face; he scowled at Jane, obviously as displeased with her chosen occupation as his parents.

"It's personal," he snapped.

"I know darling, but tell us what happened," cooed his mother, rubbing his shoulder encouragingly and warmly, "Jennie's safety may be at stake."

Steve's expression turned blank again under his mother's urging. He swallowed and took a breath, looking for all to Jane like an actor prepared to recite memorized lines.

"Jennie and I told her folks we were going to the movies, but, we didn't. We took a drive out to Pebble Creek so we could talk."

"Where exactly in Pebble Creek did you go?" asked Jane.

Steve suddenly looked flustered.

"I...I don't know. Just up to Pebble Creek, to park," he said, stumbling over his words. It appeared to Ralph and the Ballards he was confused because he wasn't sure of the location, but Jane saw it was because he really had no answer.

"Well, how far from the parking area would you say you were?" Jane said, pressing harder, "A couple of yards? A hundred yards? A mile?"

"Yeah, a mile. About a mile from the parking area. On the big hill nearest to Pebble Creek," he said swiftly.

"And what did you talk about?" Jane asked.

"We've been having fights...Jennie wanted to start seeing other guys...that we should cool it between us. I said I didn't want to. We started to argue and when I said if she started seeing other guys I was going to start seeing other girls, she got real mad, and left the car, and ran off."

"Where did she run Steve?" asked Ralph quickly, not liking that Jane appeared to have taken over his questioning.

"I don't know. She just ran off into the woods."

"Did you follow her?" asked Jane.

"I was mad too," said Steve, looking up and scowling at Jane, "I just started the car and drove around Pebble Creek till I cooled off. Then I started for home. I thought I'd see Jennie along the way, but I didn't. I figured she got a ride or was taking a short-cut home through the woods."

"And that was the last time you saw her?" asked Jane.

"Yeah."

The Ballards both nodded, Steve's explanation sounding reasonable and plausible to them, his parents. Ralph too heard the logic of Steve's story, but hearing was all he did. Jane saw and felt as well as heard, and, to her, Steve's story, what parts he was ready to recite, was too pat, too rehearsed sounding, and he especially looked too calm for a boyfriend who had just heard his girlfriend had not shown up after running off into the woods at night, even if they had just had a fight. Either he wasn't serious about Jennie, or he was lying about the whole thing to cover something else up. Jane's instincts lead her to believe the latter.

"Well, thank you Steve, for cooperating with us," said Ralph. He put on his hat. "We'll be going now. Let you people get some sleep. Deputy."

Ralph looked at Jane and headed for the door. Jane followed, putting on her hat too, but casting a glance at Steve. Like Charlie O'Brien, he too knew something he was not saying and Jane added him to Charlie as an interview to follow up on later, and alone.

Ralph took the photo of Jennie from Jane and her notes to take back to the Sheriff's office to complete the APB and write up the report after he ordered her to start patrolling Pebble Creek for the missing girl. Jane did, but on her way there, which was through town, she passed the Grangeville Chronicle's office and saw lights still on in there. Jane stopped and found Tim still busy with the next day's edition. She told him of Jennie's disappearance and recited all the facts completely even without her notes. Tim thanked her for the scoop and said he would get it in tomorrow's paper, along with a plea for any information as to the girl's whereabouts. Jane then excused herself, explaining she was ordered to patrol the Pebble Creek area.

"Good luck then," said Tim, as Jane started for the front door of the office.

"Thank you. And you hurry and finish here. It's after midnight," said Jane, taking a quick glance at her watch for the time.

Tim looked at her, contemplating her just for the briefest second before answering.

"I will," he said.

It was there on her patrol of Pebble Creek that Jane heard the call over the radio about Pops' murder the following morning. She had found nothing in the area she patrolled but then she could only cover a small section of the large area that park was composed of in the length of time that made up her shift. The end of it came right after the removal of Pops' body, and Jane then headed into Grangeville to have lunch with Butch Przybylski.

CHAPTER THREE

At twenty-five years of age, Jane Marie Fleming was not as she appeared to be, in any way. She looked quite tall and lanky, when actually she was only five feet five inches tall, and always on the lookout for any extra pounds that might sneak up on her. But her legs were long and so were her arms, giving the impression she was taller than she really was. Her shoulders were broad, as broad as someone who really was tall, which added to the illusion of her being a greater height than what she really was. She had a pretty face but the prettiness only came out when she wore make-up, and she never wore make-up while she was on duty, since she felt that would emphasize her womanhood to her fellow deputies, and she wanted to avoid doing that. And she never had any call to wear it when off-duty; Butch didn't care if she wore make-up or not, he told her he liked her any way she wanted to present herself.

If there was one outstanding, beautiful feature of Jane's, it had to be her hair. It was long, thick and luxurious and fell down her back in gentle waves, when she didn't pull it back in a simple ponytail for work. The only drawback was the color. It was a rather nondescript dishwater blond. Even her eye color was nothing to notice, it seemed to be a mishmash mixture of green and gray.

At one time Jane struggled to be beautiful, through high school and college she applied the make-up, she curled and bleached the hair. She fought back hard against the pounds. But the new wave of feminism that swelled up in the mid-sixties caught her attention and fancy, and decided to hell with it. If people were going to like and accept her, it was going to be as herself, the "plain" Jane. The irony of that thought with that expression was not lost on her, and she took it to mean what she decided to do was right. She did discover she liked better the new people she attracted as her new self, than the old friends who drifted away after she stopped painting and primping herself up. One of those included her college sweetheart, Tom Fontaine. He came right out and told her he didn't

Michele Taylor

33

appreciate her new look, and didn't think the wife of the lawyer he was planning to be should look the way she did now. Jane realized she had to choose between the image Tom wanted from her and her real self. She found it no problem to choose her real self.

After graduating from Michigan State University with a degree in psychology she decided she wanted to be a cop. A semester of criminal psychology in her senior year got her interested in dealing with controlling these people and helping the victims of them. She decided the best way was to become a cop. She went back to MSU and got a Masters degree in police science. But when it came time to find a job, she met with nothing but difficulty. Department after department in every city she applied to turned her down. The stated excuses were all different, but the underlying real reason Jane knew was because she was a woman. Finally, when Grangeville turned down her application, unluckily for it Jane decided to take action and file a suit of sexual discrimination. It was with hidden glee that she watched the city fathers squirm under the pressure of deciding whether to suffer the publicity that was brewing around Jane's suit and would rain down heavily on them should it reach the courtroom, or avoid the fight and hire her. When they decided to hire her, she savored the last amount of glee before moving into the force to face the hostility of the Sheriff and the other deputies.

This happened seven months ago, but only now, this October, was Jane finally, but grudgingly receiving some acceptance from Ralph and Galen and Clark and the other deputies. No longer was she being plagued by pranks such as pulling out her chair behind her desk and finding a sanitary napkin placed in the middle of it, and hearing Clark and Galen and some of the others snickering in the next room when she did. Ralph was never in on these pranks, at least Jane never suspected he was, but she sometimes felt it would be easier to handle if he did. Ralph's handling of her employment in the department seemed to be a hands-off policy, to act like she wasn't even there. That she found harder to handle than Clark and Galen's pranks. At least they were acknowledging she was there, if in a despicable and childish way. But Ralph kept her outside the mainstream of the police work, and she didn't like that even more than being harassed. Though she had to admit Ralph got better as time went on, so much so that she wasn't surprised when he had asked her over Clark to come with him on the O'Brien call. But she still sensed Ralph kept her out of things, and she had a hunch the reason was sexual, not professional. She had a feeling Ralph was afraid of women, that he felt threatened by them sexually. He had never married and Butch told her couldn't recall Ralph ever having a relationship with a woman during the years Butch was growing up in Grangeville. After he said that Butch grinned and said that made him feel safe to have his woman work for such a man.

But though things were better for Jane in the Sheriff's Department, they were still not perfect, and the townspeople were another story. Even now she was still being treated shabbily or harshly or contemptuously, though not enough so she could not do her job. But while she herself was not respected, the position she had was, for Grangeville believed in law and order, and her actions were accepted and her orders obeyed. Jane knew this was due to the position of deputy Sheriff, but some of this too she realized came from the fact she was Butch Przybylski's girl. And if there was a force to be reckoned with in Grangeville, a tell-it-like-it-is critic of the townspeople and their attitudes, a person who was brave enough because of his cynicism to point out stupidity and bigotry when he saw it, it was Butch Przybylski.

Jane pulled up in front of the Przybylski Garage and Filling Station, just as the noon whistle from the fire station sounded, and parked. She made a brief stop at the Chronicle's office to tell Tim of the Sylvia Griffiths lead she found in Pops' address book. Tim was in the midst of going to press so she didn't talk long, but he asked her about lunch and she told him she was meeting Butch. Jane invited Tim to join them, but he quickly said he couldn't today, since he had the paper to get out by four. Maybe some other time, he said. Jane agreed, and left, leaving Tim to pensively go back to the presses.

It had become a bright, sunny, Indian Summer afternoon, as if nothing as horrid as Pops' murder had taken place. Jane got out of the squad car, shut the door and walked up to the garage, her keys and handcuffs jangling at her hip as she walked.

The little bell on the door jangled when Jane opened the door and walked into the office area of the garage. Behind the counter stood Pete Schmidt, another mechanic at the garage. Slight in build, bespectacled, in a gray-green uniform with his name in red letters on a white patch sewn on his upper left chest, Pete looked up from his paperwork when Jane came in.

"Hi Pete," said Jane.

"Hi Deputy," Pete replied, grinning a pinched lip grin at her. Pete was one of the enlightened males of Jane's generation who had no qualms in accepting a female in a male's job. Plus, Pete was one of Butch's friends as well as employees and he liked how happy Butch was with Jane. But the grin on Pete's face disappeared a moment later. "Pretty bad about Pops," he added.

"Yes. It was not a very pleasant sight," said Jane.

"You saw it?" said Pete, in awe. Police work fascinated Pete and another reason he liked Jane was the vicarious thrill he got being close to a real law enforcement officer. "Anybody have any idea what happened?" he asked.

Jane paused thoughtfully, then shook her head.

"Nothing concrete yet, Pete," she said. Then she nodded towards the garage. "The Big Guy ready to go to lunch?"

"He's waiting for you with baited breath," teased Pete.

Jane smiled at the real warmth in Pete's voice, then walked through another doorway into the garage, in which a clanging was heard coming from under a '62 yellow Plymouth parked at the far end. Andy French, another employee at the garage, was on his way out to wait on a customer at the gas pumps and he and Jane exchanged only a smile and a nod, as the clanging got louder from under the Plymouth, punctuated now with a few choice four-letter words. Andy left and Jane walked around the car to the other side. A pair of long legs stretched out from underneath the car, legs in the same gray-green uniform as Pete's, and with feet in a pair of scruffy, battered, running shoes.

Jane smiled slightly and nudged one of the shoes with the toe of her boot.

"Hey buddy," she yelled above the clanging, "No loitering allowed."

The clanging stopped and the body attached to the legs rolled out from the car, and Butch Przybylski, owner and operator of the Przybylski Garage and Filling Station, smiled up at Jane.

The first thing anyone noticed about 33 year old Butch Przybylski was the gap-between-the-front-teeth grin that often spread across his handsome face. In other male faces such a smile made them look sweet and boyish. But in the face of Butch Przybylski such a smile lit up a devilish and manly expression, an expression that was totally truthful in the impression it made. Butch had thick, wavy, red-brown hair but very pale blond eyebrows and lashes. However, those only emphasized his shiny clear blue eyes that Jane thought put that certain movie star's famous blue eyes to shame. He had a fleshy, full face and his complexion was flatteringly ruddy. He was a tall man, six feet two, but not overpoweringly big; he possessed no large muscles but was incredibly strong, his grip was like an iron vise. Matching red-brown hair grew on the back of his hands and up his arms and some of it on his chest showed where he had his uniform and shirt underneath it open at the neck. Butch was smart, witty, and hated bullshit in any and all forms with a passion, and when aroused Butch's passion was something. He never refrained from pointing bullshit out in anyone or anything brashly and unselfconsciously. No one could ever defend themselves intelligently against his remarks. Those who tried came off on the short end and looked ridiculous at best, stupid at the worst. Because he "butchered" his foes so savagely was the reason he got the nickname Butch, and there were few in Grangeville who even remembered or called him by his real name, which was Michael.

"Yeah, I know," he said, "But I'm in good with the cops around here."

He got up gracefully. Butch towered over Jane, being over six feet, so when he kissed her he as always lifted her slightly on her toes with his arm that he slipped around her back.

When he lingered in the kiss Jane turned her face slightly and tried to pull away, but was unsuccessful.

"Butch, please," she whispered, though there was a touch of reluctance in it.

"Oh yeah, I keep forgetting, you have to keep up an official appearance while on duty." He released her. "But everybody knows about us." He leaned down to her ear and whispered melodramatically: "And even that we actually have sex together!"

Butch rolled his eyes in mock horror, making Jane laugh softly. He went to the workbench and put away his wrench, then began to wash his hands in the sink.

"So someone did in ol' Pops Griffiths, huh?" he said as he lathered up.

"How did you hear? I even had Pete mention it."

"Huh! You know nothing happens here that the news doesn't spread like wildfire. Someone farts wrong in this town and in an hour everybody knows it."

Butch rinsed his hands and began drying them on some paper towels as Jane watched him intently.

"You never did like Pops, did you?" she said.

"No I didn't," said Butch, bluntly and contemptuously, "Everyone else in this town may have thought he was a living saint, but I thought he was a son-of-a-bitch." Butch crumbled up the towels into a ball and tossed it into a barrel.

"I can't say I liked him or not. I never had that much association with him. Till now." Jane's expression became ironic for a moment. "But I got the impression the few times I did see him he wasn't too pleased with a female deputy Sheriff on the force."

"He probably wasn't," stated Butch firmly, "He was an ornery ol' bastard."

"What did he do that makes you feel this way?" asked Jane.

"Oh, he was a pain in my ass ever since I was a little kid. He'd crab that I was eating too much candy and tell me my teeth would all rot and fall out, or I was a snotty little boy and would burn in hell when I died. And it didn't stop when I grew up and opened this place. He'd complain he wasn't waited on fast enough, or he'd bring in that pile of junk he drove and expect me to fix it, even after I told him it was almost beyond repair and he should get a new car. Well, heaven forbid he should spend any of his money on a new car, or pay the amount I would charge him to fix the old one. He'd say I was charging too much and that he wasn't going to give me all that. But he did, because I said I would lock the car up in the garage if he didn't. I didn't mind all this bickering so much, but then he'd start in on me, telling me I was a cheat and a swindler and a liar and a lousy mechanic!" Butch said the last two words with mock outrage so Jane laughed again, loudly. "Call me a liar and call me a cheat and call me a swindler, but like hell if I'll like anyone who called me a lousy mechanic!"

Jane laughed completely right out loud and Butch grinned. He walked up to Jane and put his arm around her shoulders.

"C'mon. I'm starved. Let's go get something to eat."

Butch's opinion of Pops reinforced Jane's theory about who killed him and the circumstances surrounding his death. She tucked Butch's opinion in the back of her mind for now as the two of them walked across the street to have lunch at Ma's Cafe.

***

Jane met Butch not long after she won her fight to be hired by the Sheriff's Department. Butch was living with his friend Sy McIntire at the time. She was patrolling the back roads past the high school and football field on an early spring night when, above the grind of the gravel under the patrol car's tires she heard the high pitched whine that comes from a stereo blasting out music. Houses were a good distance apart in this area but Jane was concerned that the noise might disturb some of the older neighbors. Better to check into the situation before it became a problem.

Also, at the time she jumped at any chance to prove herself capable of being a deputy Sheriff and handling the job.

She followed the noise till she came to a small ranch-style house set back about a hundred yards from the road. Though the house was set back that far, Jane could now hear the music coming from it clearly, and it was the most recent Rolling Stones album. She stopped the car in the driveway and rolled down her window, looking at the house, her expression incredulous. Then she drove on, up the house.

The lawn was well cared for, the grass mowed and very green, even a few begonias flowered in a row in front of the porch. Two cars were parked before a garage, two '71 Mustangs that were obviously well taken care of. Jane parked in the horseshoe driveway right in the middle, right in front of the house. She turned off her headlights and shut off the car. There was still no sign of the occupants of the house as she got out of the car, putting on her hat and slamming the door. Obviously the music deafened the people inside to her outside completely. Bright yellow light came flooding out of the large picture window next to the front door. Jane glanced in it before she knocked on the door and was surprised to see a very neat living room. She pounded on the screen door hard with her knuckles.

To her surprise the heavy wooden door opened only a few seconds later. A very cute, dark-haired, tall, skinny young man appeared at the door. He was in jeans and a local softball team shirt. In his hand was a mug half-filled with beer. Immediately when he saw Jane, he looked wary.

"Oh, oh," he said.

"Excuse me sir," yelled Jane, "But I'm afraid I'm going to have to ask you to turn down your stereo."

"Oh, yeah, sure. We didn't realize..." said the man loudly. He looked to be about Jane's age, perhaps a little older, in his early to mid thirties. To Jane's further surprise he opened the screen door. "C'mon in," he said.

Jane stepped in past the man as he held the door open for her. She took off her hat while she got a better look around the room. It was neat, as she noticed before, but simple. A sofa and two chairs, all mismatched, lined

the two sides of the room. Mismatched lamps sat on matching end tables.
A larger coffee table, before a fireplace, held a Scrabble board in the midst
of a game, some of the tiles were scattered about on it. The stereo where
the music bellowed out was in a comer next to the fireplace.

"Hey Butch!" yelled the man behind her at the door, towards a hallway
opposite it, "We got company!"

The man then realized his job might be easier if he turned down the
volume of the music, and quickly scurried to the stereo to do so.

Jane took a few steps into the room as he did. Just after she did a figure
came into the room from the hallway. It was Butch.

Jane turned towards him at his appearance. He was also in jeans but
instead of a softball shirt, he wore an obnoxiously loud patterned
short-sleeved shirt. He was pouring a can of beer into a large frosted mug.
A German Shepherd-looking mutt trotted in at his heels and immediately
started to bark in short, gruff yaps at the sight of Jane.

"Hey Sy, why'd ja turn down the stereo?" said Butch. He saw Jane and
stopped pouring the beer. Then slowly his wicked grin crossed his face. It
was right then that Jane got hooked on Michael David "Butch"
Przybylski.

"Oh. I see why," said Butch. He looked down at the dog next to him,
who was still emitting short barks. "Jesse, shut up. Can't you see it's the
law?" he said firmly, and just as quickly as he started Jesse stopped barking,
but remained eagerly alert to the new arrival.

"I guess we didn't realize how loud we put it," said the man by the
stereo, "Sorry Deputy."

"Fine," Jane replied to him, but still looked at Butch.

"So you're the new female deputy," said Butch, coming into the room
and setting down his beer can and mug on one of the end tables, Jesse following at his heels. "We've heard a lot about you." He held out his hand to
Jane. "I'm Butch Przybylski."

"Jane Fleming," said Jane, and she shook Butch's hand. He grasped her hand in his strong one and squeezed it while they shook. Jane gave his a squeeze just before they let go of their grasp.

"I happen to be Sy McIntire," said Sy at the stereo. He eyed Jane and Butch eyeing each other. "In case anyone wants to know."

Jane looked up at him, startled. "Oh, how do you do?" And she shook hands with Sy, briefly.

"I don't suppose we can offer you a beer," said Sy.

"No," said Jane, turning her head to take a look at Butch, then turning back to Sy. "But thanks for the offer, anyway."

"Maybe some other time?" said Butch, as Jane walked to the door. Jesse, picking up on his master's approval of Jane, followed her to the door and offered his big head to her to be petted. Jane stopped at the door and looked back at Butch after stroking Jesse on the head.

"Definitely some other time," she said.

The sparks began flying between Butch and Jane right then, and continued stronger the next day when Jane had to bring in her patrol car to the Przybylski Garage for its regular oil change and met Butch again. Discovering his intolerance for bullshit and don't-give-a-damn attitude about what other people thought made him very appealing to Jane, and her obstinate nature in bucking the system to get the job of deputy Sheriff had made Jane appealing to Butch even before he had met her. They arranged to meet for pizza and beer at Uncle Nunzio's Pizzeria on Main Street that night, and from that date, their affair began.

The sexual side of their affair ran into a problem when it came to finding a place to make love so they might be discreet for Jane's sake as a deputy. Jane rented the apartment above the Grangeville Five & Dime and Pharmacy. Several dates after their first at Uncle Nunzio's the physical attraction between them got too strong to put off anymore, and they went back to Jane's apartment. Jane closed the shades and locked the door, but the room wasn't soundproof and Butch's Mustang was parked in front at the curb all night. Whispers about the two spread through the town like wildfire the next day. Butch didn't give a damn about it, but was sensitive to Jane's distress stemming from her position as deputy, and the first and only female one as well. She didn't want to give the townspeople more ammunition against her. So even though the initial damage was done, they agreed not to sleep together in Jane's apartment again.

But Butch's house wasn't much of a solution either. Location-wise his house was excellent, but then there was the matter of Sy. The house belonged to Butch, having inherited it from his grandmother who had lived in Grangeville till her death. But Sy had lived with Butch and paid his rent promptly way before Jane had arrived in town and was a good friend, so Butch found it difficult to think of asking him to move out. When Sy went on vacation to Colorado for two weeks it was perfect for Jane and Butch, but still Butch couldn't bring himself to ask Sy to move. However, Sy, ever perceptive, noticing the attraction between Butch and Jane and their dilemma, soon announced he was moving out of Butch's house and in with Pete Schmidt. Butch tried to talk him out of it, but Sy, liking Butch and liking Jane and liking them both together, could not be made to change his mind. He teased Butch, saying Pete was charging him way less rent than Butch, and Pete's mother was going to do his laundry for him too.

Now Butch and Jane had enough privacy, but appearances still had to be worried about. This was 1972 but this was also rock hard conservative Grangeville. A couple sleeping together was one thing, but to live together without the benefit of wedlock was another. Jane knew that would be pushing the town's tolerance too far. Butch wanted Jane to move in with him, but again respected how important the pubic attitude towards Jane was to her functioning as a law enforcement officer. So Jane didn't move in completely with Butch, but for all intent and purpose she did. She had most of her belongings and spent most of her nights there. But the apartment in town was still hers so no one could say she was openly, completely, living in sin with Butch.

Jane had gone off the Pill in college, and after graduation had continued on it, though she and Tom had broken up, since she felt no adverse effects to it and it did away with the bad menstrual cramps she used to get. But as for taking it for birth control, she'd had no sexual relationship after Tom until Butch.

Butch was devil-may-care out in public, but alone with Jane he showed his deep vulnerability. He was a sweet, considerate lover, but still there were occasional flashes of his cynicism in his moves that spiced their lovemaking and excited Jane. And his stamina was incredible. Jane once told him as they lay gasping for breath after a particularly robust session that he had the lasting power of ten men. Butch's reply was he was kind of nasty once and awhile but he made up for it by being real healthy.

There was also a comfortableness with Butch, in mind, body, and soul, that she never felt with any other man before. It would have been right for Jane with any of the other men she previously was involved with, but with Butch, she met her soul mate. She knew there was never going to be as important a man in her life as Butch if she ever split with him. As well as liking him, and loving him, she soon was cherishing him as well, and the time they spent together. But despite their closeness Jane was not completely sure Butch felt the exact same way she did. He told her often that he loved her, and his lovemaking was genuine, but there was still a small spot of doubt on Jane's self-esteem that made her slightly unsure of the intensity of Butch's feelings. Because he was her soul mate it was easy for Jane to talk to Butch, but not about this. In everything else though.

Butch was a sympathetic listener to her daily problems and the incidents of prejudice she faced as Grangeville's female deputy, and always knew what to say to put everything in perspective and make her feel better. There were times when Jane felt she couldn't take anymore and was ready to give up and quit, but a talk with Butch and she was ready for the next time to handle whoever would hassle her and give them solid hell.

They crossed Main Street and entered Ma's Cafe. Lunchtime was well underway and others were already served and halfway through their meals.

The gentle clink of silverware against plates and the soft rumble of different conversations filled the air. There was a slight pause in the clinks and conversations as Butch and Jane walked in, but soon resumed when they walked to a booth by the front window and sat. The lulls in conversations were greater and more noticeable when Jane first became deputy and she walked in, but after Butch spent his first night with Jane and they walked in together the lull was like a dead weight in the air. Jane felt uncomfortable and struggled with dealing with the silence, but Butch only stared down the looks and silence with annoyance. He looked one diner right in the eye and declared loudly: "What's the matter? The food gotten cold or something?" The diner squirmed slightly in his seat and glanced, devastated, around the restaurant. Slowly everyone went back to their meals and Butch directed Jane to the middle booth right next to the big windows overlooking Main Street. That became their regular seats each time they came in to Ma's for lunch.

"How's my favorite crime fighter, and the bum she wastes her time with?" Waitress Gracie White approached Butch and Jane's table with two tall glasses of ice water. Gracie was a stout, short woman, as forthright and blunt as Butch. She was a pretty woman in her late thirties and always reminded Jane of a stack of pink marshmallows in her pink, lacy waitress uniform. Gracie was the one person besides Butch and his friends who had supported Jane when she first announced she was becoming a deputy Sheriff, and the only person besides Butch's friends who did not disapprove of the extent of Butch and Jane's relationship. In fact, she thought it was just great, and loudly declared so one day in the restaurant not long after it started. Butch and Jane were amused and knew they had found a strong ally in Gracie.

She set a glass of water in front of each of them and pulled the pencil from its position in her pinned up brown hair near her ear and poised it above her order pad. Butch and Jane grinned at her.

"I keep telling you Gracie, dump your old man and kids and I'll show you just how much Janie is wasting her time," said Butch, as he drew out a small cigar from his uniform pocket and lit it. Gracie rolled her eyes in mock horror while Butch grinned wickedly.

"I'd do that but I got a load of laundry to do tonight," said Gracie. Jane laughed, secure enough in her relationship with Butch to always be amused at the innuendoes and raunchy banter between Butch and Gracie.

"What would you two like today?" asked Gracie.

"I'll have the turkey sandwich. With lettuce and tomato, on whole wheat bread, and hold the mayo this time, will you Gracie?" said Jane.

"You don't got it," said Gracie, writing the order down.

"And a cup of coffee," added Jane. Gracie nodded.

"And how about you, lover?" Gracie asked Butch.

"A double cheeseburger and a double order of fries, give me a bowl of chili and an extra large chocolate shake and a piece of apple pie. A la mode," ordered Butch from the menu while puffing on his cigar.

Gracie's brows came together when she finished writing down Butch's order.

"How does this man stay so skinny when he eats like a horse?" Gracie said to Jane.

"I wish I knew Gracie," said Jane, looking over at Butch enviously. Butch smiled very self-satisfied, smoke drifting out from his mouth.

"Hey, did I hear right Jane? Has Jennie O'Brien really been reported missing?" asked Gracie suddenly, amazed. Jane nodded.

"I've been assigned to the investigation. You didn't by chance see her anytime last night did you? Did she and her boyfriend happen to come in here?" Jane asked.

"Nope. I was working last night too. Didn't notice her coming in." Gracie shook her head, resting her fist on her considerable hip. "God, having two things like this happen at the same time. Pops' murder and Jennie turning up missing." Gracie shuddered and walked off to holler in Butch's and Jane's orders to the cook in the kitchen. Jane watched her a moment, then turned back to Butch who had been watching and listening to her and Gracie.

"Somebody turned up missing?" asked Butch.

"You didn't hear that?" asked Jane.

"Nope. That I didn't hear. I guess this town's grapevine isn't as hot as I thought. Who did Gracie say is missing?"

"Jennie O'Brien."

Butch shook his head slightly in non-recognition.

"The Sheriff and I talked to her boyfriend last night. Steve Ballard."

This name brought a recognizing expression to Butch's face.

"Oh yeah, I know Steve. Was in a couple times with his car. What did he have to stay?"

"They took a drive out to Pebble Creek to talk, they got into a fight and Jennie got mad and ran off," said Jane.

"And nobody's seen her since, huh?" Butch shook his head. "Doesn't sound too good to me."

Jane nodded in agreement. She then leaned her elbows on the table and rested her head on her hands suddenly. Butch quickly set aside his cigar in the ashtray and reached over to take one of Jane's hands, pulling it across the table to him. He held it tenderly, his big one covering hers completely.

"You look awfully tired, honey," he said quietly and gently. Jane nodded again, letting the fatigue show through completely on her face now.

"I was out all night patrolling Pebble Creek looking for the O'Brien girl," she replied.

"You want to cancel our weekend at the LaPierre?" Butch asked.

Jane looked stunned at his words.

"Oh no," she said quickly, " I'll just go home and catch a few hours of sleep before we leave," she added casually. Then she dropped her voice in tone and volume to a husky growl. " I don't want to miss our LaPierre weekend."

Butch grinned wickedly. "That's my woman," he said, also giving her a wicked wink.

"Do you think I'd let a little fatigue get in the way of a weekend of decadence at the LaPierre?"

Butch raised his eyebrows in mock horror at her words but also grinned again approvingly. He then let go of Jane's hand and they sat back in the booth.

"So what do you think happened to this O'Brien girl?" asked Butch, picking up his cigar and taking a long draw on it.

Jane sat a moment before speaking. She dropped her voice to whisper again, in all seriousness this time.

"Butch, I think there's a link between Pops' death and Jennie's disappearance," she said.

Immediately Butch looked alert and terribly interested.

"What?" he asked eagerly in a whisper.

But Jane spotted Gracie coming with her coffee and Butch's chocolate shake just then, and shook her head.

"I'll tell you later," she whispered, "I'll tell you exactly what I think happened."

CHAPTER FOUR

Jane caught a few hours of sleep before Butch got off work, dropped Jesse off at Pete's for Pete to take care of, and arrived at her apartment to pick her up for the trip up north. He used his key to her apartment and was sitting on the edge of her bed when she turned around and woke to find Butch smiling down at her. The mid-afternoon sun's rays came through the cracks in the venetian blinds covering her bedroom windows, illuminating the small room with warm golden light. The light set off Butch's pale eyebrows and lashes and set his red hair glowing. In her half-sleep state he looked so incredibly desirable to Jane that she reached up and pulled his head down to hers and kissed him. The room was so warmly lit and the bed so comfortably soft they broke their rule of not making love in Jane's apartment, and ended up not leaving Grangeville for the LaPierre till an hour later than they planned. Driving down Main Street, they passed the newsstands containing the Grangeville Chronicle with its headline announcing Pops' murder and it's article about Jennie O'Brien's disappearance. They passed the Chronicle's office and Tim happened to be looking out just then, and he saw them pass by in Butch's Mustang.

The LaPierre Motel was just outside little Remus, Michigan. Butch discovered it one year when he went hunting with a cousin who lived there. Butch and his cousin Joe drove past it on their way farther north and Butch was impressed with the seclusion of the quaint little ten unit motel. It was situated at the end of a 90 degree bend in the road, just before the road made another 90 degree bend heading back in its original direction, so it appeared the little motel was tucked away unobtrusively in a corner. But what really impressed Butch, and sold him on the motel as a great getaway, he saw on the return journey. It was late at night and he and Joe were driving south towards the LaPierre. The road rose to a slight hill and then dropped somewhat abruptly. The slight hill blocked the view down the road till they were at the top of the incline, so Butch did not see the LaPierre till then. But when he did, it was a sight to behold.

All along the edge of the roof ran neon lights: a double string of hot pink neon that glowed vibrantly in the darkness. The name was also written out in hot pink neon on the front of the main building, as well as the word "vacancy" which at the time was lit too. And the lights coming into view so abruptly heightened its shock twice as much. Butch let out a long admiring whistle as Joe drove by the LaPierre.

"My goodness, ain't that sumthin'," said Butch.

"What's that?" asked Joe, turning the steering wheel.

"This LaPierre Motel," said Butch, nodding at it. Joe took a quick glance at it and grinned.

"It looks me like its just sitting there waiting for someone to come along and do something sweaty and decadent with somebody else in it," said Butch, as the lights disappeared behind them.

So much of an impression the motel made on Butch that when he met Jane, and the problem of privacy for their lovemaking came up, but before Sy solved it, Butch took Jane up to the LaPierre Motel for a weekend.

That weekend the La Pierre provided just what Butch imagined it would. It was a hot May evening when Jane and Butch pulled up to the motel bathed in the gleaming hot pink neon light. Jane was similarly impressed by the LaPierre's ambiance. Butch checked them in. They entered their room, and except for ventures out for food, did not come out till checkout time Sunday.

It was a tiny, comfortable, romantically decorated room. But they did not spend much time looking around it. That sense of checking into a motel for illicit reasons seem to take over them the moment they shut the door. The room was a little warm because the air conditioning hadn't been turned on yet, it being only May still. The warmth seemed to wrap around them as they lowered themselves on the bed, locked in an embrace and a kiss. Even after Sy moved out, Butch and Jane still went to the LaPierre occasionally.

It was close to nine o'clock before Butch and Jane drove up to the LaPierre this night in October. Butch checked them in while Jane brought out their small suitcases from the back seat of Butch's car. Butch returned only moments later, their checking in pretty routine by now, the manager familiar with Mr. and Mrs. Butch Przybylski.

Butch unlocked the door to Unit 4, the unit farthest from the office and their regular room, with the key and walked in, Jane following. He switched on the light and the room sprang into view. Jane set the suitcases down while Butch shut the door. As he did Jane switched the light back off, and the only light was that which filtered through the drawn blinds from the neon. Butch looked puzzled at Jane in the dimness.

"Janie, honey, I thought we agreed to settle in and then get something to eat..." But his sentence was cut off as Jane stepped up to him and kissed him hard and full.

"Just where did you learn to do that?" he then asked.

"My mother used to do that to me, when she tucked me in bed, after she kissed me goodnight. I don't know where she got the idea, but, I always felt happy after she did it."

"Me too," said Butch, and he smiled slightly.

Jane leaned down and their lips met in a gentle kiss that quickly intensified. Slowly Jane slipped down till her legs were on the outer sides of his. In the back of her mind she was grateful she had taken the time to shave her legs this morning so they were silkily smooth. It never failed to arouse Butch when they were and she rubbed them against his own heavily hairy ones. She did so and sure enough, she felt him become hard and erect.

"You vicious, wanton, wicked, woman, you," muttered Butch, but the look in his eyes was amused.

"Yeah, I got your number buster," whispered back Jane and she grinned, "I know your buttons to push."

They rolled again on their sides and their arms slid around each other in a tight embrace. Their breaths started to come rapid and heavy.

"Butch. Butch," said Jane softly. She now snaked her legs around his long, lanky, sturdy ones, trying to get as close to him as possible. At a time like this, Jane felt a part of Butch. And she was sure he felt the same way too.

"Janie," he whispered back. Carefully he snaked his fingers up through her thick hair and tightened his fingers around strands of it. Suddenly he pulled her head by her hair backwards, gently but firmly, and Jane went on her back. Butch followed on top of her. Using the leverage her legs wrapped around his gave him, he pulled her legs apart and slowly began to enter her.

"Oh Butch. Butch." Jane began to repeat his name between clenched teeth. Violent waves of sensation bubbled up through her whole body from the point of her contact with Butch. She clutched at his broad back in tighter and tighter embraces as he got closer and closer to entering her completely. Deep grunting breaths began to emit from Butch. Then with a deeply emitted breath Butch completed his journey. Jane let out a groan and Butch then started to rock up and down, so forcefully the bed also began to bounce and even slightly bang up against the wall.

In the back part of her mind which was not a massive swirl of ecstatic emotions like the rest of it Jane was amazed at the staying power of Butch. It felt like he could do this all night and half the next day and not give out. But sweat did begin to appear on his body and caused him to slide a little against Jane. He had his head buried over her shoulder in the pillow and his cheek next to hers began to dampen it with sweat too. The little gut noises he then began to make echoed loudly in Jane's ear. Soon she began to rock up and down against his rhythm, and it took only a few seconds of all this to evoke a wild orgasm in Jane. Her eyes shut and her head rocked back and forth in a frenzy, and her hair whipped around her face. After several minutes her reaction subsided and her mouth dropped open, and she breathed heavily through it, gasping noises accompanying each intake of air. This slowly returned to normal too and her heart slowed its thudding in her ears. She moved her head straight and opened her eyes to look at Butch. He was grinning down at her, thoroughly enjoying himself. Jane stared up at him blankly, her ebbed emotions not yet returned from the outer spheres her orgasm took them. But like a tidal wave they rushed back and with a vicious smirk Jane jerked forcefully the lower part of her body first to the right and then to the left. They had discovered this action made Butch come and the technique did not fail now.

Jane snuggled next to Butch as he laid down while still regaining his breath and calming. She was grinning wickedly when he finally looked at her.

"I thought we agreed last time that you would warn me before you 'Cracked the Whip'."

"I agreed nothing. *You* mentioned the warning stuff." Jane leaned up on Butch to lay face to face with him. "It's that element of surprise that's half the secret to its success."

They kissed deeply, Butch's strong fingers creeping through Jane's hair to her head again.

***

An hour and a half later Butch and Jane sat in bed having pizza and beer. The pizza was ordered from a nearby pizzeria, which usually did not supply beer, but Butch convinced the owner to have the delivery man stop and buy him a six pack too. The delivery man was already out anyway, Butch reasoned to the pizzeria owner, and what would be the point of having a pizza delivered if he, Butch, had to go out for the beer? It was impossible for anyone to say no to Butch or his logic, so each time Butch called for a pizza, a six pack of beer was delivered along with it.

Butch sat up in bed, with his pants on, having had to put them on to take delivery of the pizza and beer. Jane sat next to him wearing his flannel shirt. She flipped up the lid *of* the pizza carton and took out another slice.

"*Another* slice?" said Butch.

"I haven't eaten since lunch time," said Jane defensively.

"Yes. Now I remember that," said Butch, taking a sip from his can of beer while Jane took a bite of the pizza slice.

"I have to admit I feel a little guilty about this weekend," said Jane.

"Finally. What did we do? So we can do it again next time," said Butch.

Jane laughed, then became serious. "No. I mean, I feel guilty about leaving town with a murder and a disappearance hanging over it. Especially since I'm in charge of the disappearance investigation."

"Who's taking care of it while you're gone?" asked Butch.

"Galen. "

"Galen!" Butch said annoyed, "Well, that girl will still be missing when you get back. Besides, you've worked ten days straight without a day off. You deserve this weekend. And this sounds like the perfect time to get the hell out of town anyway."

Jane looked at Butch a touch curious.

"Butch, if you don't like Grangeville, why do you stay there?"

Butch grinned, took a bite of his slice of pizza, chewed it, and swallowed.

"There are things that drive me crazy about the place, but more than driving me crazy, they amuse me."

"Amuse you?"

"It's so ridiculous the way those people in that town act. Take your case, for instance. Someone would think you're breaking the law instead of swearing to enforce it, the way people act towards you." Butch reached down and squeezed Jane's hand. "I don't mean to say I'm getting a laugh out of the way you're treated, honey."

"Oh, I know that."

"But to watch those people...it amazes me. They're such hypocrites. You don't know them like I do, I grew up there." Butch finished his beer. "So that's why I stay. Besides, where would I go? It's the same everywhere, to some degree."

Butch finished his pizza and wiped his fingers on a napkin. He sat for a minute watching Jane eat her pizza slice.

"You gonna eat that whole slice?" Butch then asked, eyeing Jane by turning slightly on his side.

"Yeah. Why?"

Jane looked at Butch curiously, chewing the bite of pizza in her mouth. Butch's wicked grin spread across his face slowly, but Jane got his message quickly. She tossed the slice back in the carton and grinned wickedly herself as she raised her arms to embrace Butch, who leaned into them. Butch also reached one hand down to his pants and deftly undid them. Jane pumped her legs up and down to push back the sheet and blankets with her feet. She also slid down to her back. Butch moved down over her and Jane spread her legs apart to cradle him. Butch kissed Jane deeply and hard. It aroused Jane to a fever pitch and she panted heavily when Butch released the kiss. He poised his mouth above hers.

"I love you Janie. Very much," he whispered.

***

Butch slept on his side, his back bare, the blankets having slipped from his shoulders. He slept oblivious to the sound of water as Jane took a morning shower. The room was brighter as the sunshine pierced through the blinds and curtains. Butch stirred slightly, then stilled.

The sound of water stopped, and Jane came out of the bathroom, wrapped in a towel. She pulled off a shower cap, tossing it aside and shaking her hair free. She saw Butch still sleeping, and smiled. She walked up quietly to the bed, then laid smiling behind Butch and leaned over his shoulder and pressed her lips against his ear.

"Buuuuutch," she cooed.

"Mmmmmmmmm," he responded.

Jane struggled up closer to him.

"Butch," she repeated softly.

Butch stirred a little, waking up slightly.

"Jane?" he mumbled.

"Who else?" she said disgruntled, then she smiled as a slight smile crossed Butch's face.

"What do you want?" he said, his eyes still closed.

"Let's play 'Cowboys and Indians'," said Jane.

"What and what?" came from Butch.

"Cowboys and Indians. I'll be the cowboy." Jane lifted her head from Butch's ear. "And you be the Indian!" she screeched and then patted her mouth while howling.

Butch's eyes sprang open as Jane continued her Indian call. He rolled onto his back and Jane leaned over him grinning.

"Good morning," she said.

Jane climbed onto Butch, one leg on each side of him. She kissed him hard and ran her fingers through his wavy hair till she reached the crown of his head, where she pulled it. Butch laid passive till she did that, and he wrapped his arms around her waist and kissed her back.

Jane raised herself slightly on one knee and positioned herself to take Butch. She held back a moment to rub her other leg against his. She sensed Butch grow larger and heard him groan.

"Oh for God's sake Janie, I ain't got the strength this morning to stand much! Do it!"

With one, sure, swift, downwards movement, she took him in and began bouncing up and down.

"Yah hoo! Ride 'em Cowboy!" shrieked Jane happy.

This was Butch's reaction that Jane thoroughly enjoyed watching. Each time his eyes rolled back into his head and his head slid backwards so his chin jutted upwards. Sometimes Jane would bite or suck his chin when it was like that, but this time she only watched him twist and roll his head ecstatically. This would start Jane to orgasm, and she would begin to force Butch deeper and deeper into herself and this time she dropped her head backwards as it went from side to side, causing the ends of her long hair to brush against Butch's legs behind her. By the time she was capable of raising her head and did so, Butch was slowly bringing his head forward too.

While Butch took his shower Jane went out and bought breakfast- She had it set up on the bed when Butch came out of the bathroom, a towel wrapped around his slim waist and his hair wet and slicked back. He sniffed the air as he walked to the bed.

"God, that coffee smells great," he said sitting on the bed opposite Jane with the breakfast laid out between them. Jane handed him a styrofoam cup filled with black coffee and took off the cover of the bacon and eggs breakfast she got from the restaurant nearby.

"Mmmmmm, I'm starving too," added Butch, picking up a plastic fork and virtually attacking the food

"I'd be surprised if we both weren't," said Jane, eagerly eating her bacon and eggs too. She grinned wickedly and Butch paused in his eating long enough to return the smile in the same way.

"I got a funny look from the guy in the next unit when I left this morning," Jane said, sipping her coffee.

"Funny? How, funny?" asked Butch.

"Well, like, we were kinda…loud, last night and this morning."

Butch laid his fork on his plate, picked up his coffee cup and took a sip.

"Oh really," he said, "Well, he better watch out when we 'Break the Sound Barrier'."

Jane stacked up the paper plates and crumpled up the Styrofoam cups before dumping them in the wastebasket. She then turned around back to the bed and unzipped her jeans, dropping them to the floor.

Slowly she walked back to the bed where Butch was sitting up leaning against the headboard, puffing on a small cigar, still wearing just the towel around his waist but his hair now dry. Puffing on the cigar, he watched Jane approach the bed and kneel on it, his flannel shirt she wore hanging down to her knees. Butch took a last puff on the cigar, then ground it out on the ashtray on the night stand next to the bed.

He rose to his knees to kneel face to face with Jane. Despite his previous words, Butch moved slowly and quietly. He slid his arms around Jane and held her tenderly. Jane slid her arms under his and up his bare back. They leaned their heads gently against each other for several minutes, not moving, just feeling the other beloved person's body in intimate contact with their own. Jane ran one of her hands up and down Butch's back, while Butch let out a deep sigh and tightened his embrace around Jane.

Butch moved his head back, prompting Jane to do the same, so they were face to face again. Repeatedly they placed small kisses on each other's lips. Then they held a kiss, drawing it art long, leisurely and tenderly.

"It's awfully pretty outside Butch," Jane whispered when they released the kiss. Their mouths were poised just a hair's width away, Jane's head tilted backwards while Butch's loomed over it. Their eyes bore into each other's. "When I went to get the breakfasts, I noticed the trees are really beautiful. Maybe we should take a walk, later."

"I think what I'm looking at right now is really beautiful," said Butch huskily. Then a flash of his famous bluntness lashed out from him. "And we definitely should fuck right now."

In one lightning fast split second Butch pushed Jane down on her back while following down on top of her while he whipped off the towel around his waist. It landed on the floor next to the bed. And Butch proceeded to "Break the Sound Barrier" on Jane, with both her utter consent and desire. The man from the next door unit who saw Jane that morning was checking out and entering his car when he heard a combination of a shriek from a woman and a yell from a man from the unit beside his. He looked at the door to the room in slight disbelief and then got into his car and drove off.

Morning passed into noontime and noon slowly drifted into afternoon. The beautiful autumn trees surrounding the LaPierre swayed in the breezes that came up and then faded out during the day. The sun began to be obscured by some rain-heavy clouds that started coming in from the north, so by mid-afternoon the threat of rain hung over the sky. A few raindrops fell in scatters over the area.

Inside Unit 4 Jane lay on Butch's chest, her eyes lightly closed and a small smile on her face. Butch lay smoking another cigar, slowly and with great deliberation. He exhaled and blew a long cloud of smoke above his and Jane's head.

A deep rumble of thunder rolled overhead, Waiting Jane and making her open her eyes. She looked up slightly and smiled.

"Oh good," she said, "It's going to rain."

"Why are you happy about that?" asked Butch, holding the cigar carefully away from Jane, "We won't be able to take that walk you wanted."

"That's okay," she said, turning her head and kissing Butch's chest repeatedly, "I like being in bed with you when it's raining."

She proceeded to kiss Butch's chest up to his face, where they exchanged several kisses. Jane then slipped down to Butch's side opposite of where he held his cigar. She watched him as he took another long draw on it.

"Does that really taste better after sex?" she asked.

"What?" asked Butch.

"That old saying. A smoke after sex. Is it better?" Jane motioned at his cigar with a small nod.

"Well, yes, I enjoy it more." Butch scrutinized the cigar. "It has to be a result of the sex." Butch looked down at Jane, who was looking at the cigar.

"Then let me see if I like it better," said Jane, grabbing it from Butch's fingers.

"Hey Janie, you don't smoke," said Butch with concern. But Jane ignored him and took a draw on the cigar. Immediately she began to cough and sputter and quickly handed it back to Butch.

"Still as repulsive as ever," she said.

Butch chuckled as Jane made a face and shook her head. Just as he took another draw on the cigar and Jane regained her breath another clap of thunder sounded overhead, deeper and stronger and closer than before.

"Ooooo, sounds like its gonna be a heavy one," said Jane. She snuggled down next to Butch. He smiled and embraced her with his free arm. Just as Butch finished the cigar, the downpour began.

The rainstorm lasted all afternoon and evening, stopping only very late that right. The thunder still rumbled, only now in the opposite direction from where it came, slowly fading. Large drops of rain dripped from the eaves of the roof steady.

His head on Jane's shoulder, Butch's breathing came steadily as he slept. The expression on his face was one of sweet repose, innocent and boyish, the complete opposite of the one when he was awake. With his eyes closed Jane could see how pale his eyelashes were, as they rested against this ruddy skin.

Jane laid awake watching Butch sleep. Carefully she stroked his hair at the side of his head with the hand she had embraced around it, so as not to wake him.

Jane had never imagined it would ever be like this, what she had with Butch. In fact, she never imagined she would ever have anything at all, again, after her breakup in college. She was emotionally dead inside, after Tom, and never believed she would feel anything for a man again. But along came Butch, and once again, her heart soared and the world seemed colored with happiness. But this was the last time. If it didn't work out with Butch, she'd never love again. Butch was the man she'd love and be devoted to forever, and if she had no life with Butch, she'd have no life with a man at all.

With him so intimately close, she allowed herself to think what would happen to her if Butch ever did leave her. A dull ache entered her heart and she shut her eyes in pain. Oh, how could she bear it if Butch ever called it off, or worse yet, found someone else? She knew she'd bear it, but she also knew the agony would be excruciating. Butch stirred a little against her; which made her open her eyes and look down at him. Slowly she smiled as reassurance came back at the sight of him. She had nothing to fear about losing Butch. They were too much alike, too similar, in tastes, outlooks and opinions, things that sealed them so closely there were no cracks in which to insert a lever to force them apart. But then her mind began to dwell on the idea they were too much alike, that as well as like gravitating towards like, opposites attracted too and maybe Butch might find someone completely different from her. Just then though Butch stirred again and woke up, and immediately grabbed Jane and kissed her, not allowing her to think further about that anymore.

The next morning, the rain having stopped and the sun increasingly piercing through the clouds it was now Butch who watched Jane sleep. She laid on her side and daintily had her hands, one on top of the other, under her cheek. Butch sat up next to her, in just his jeans, one arm leaning on his knee bent up in front of him. He watched her till she stirred and woke.

"Good morning," he said.

"Good morning," Jane said sleepily, as she sat up clutching the blankets and sheet to her. Butch reached down and brought up a Styrofoam cup of coffee and handed it to Jane.

"Thank you," she said, taking it. Butch reached down and brought up a waxed bag and held it before Jane.

"A dozen fresh glazed donuts," he said.

Not having any dinner the previous night they devoured the donuts. Butch especially. Jane ate two but Butch finished off the rest of them. Jane watched him half in envy and half in amazement.

"Where do you put all that?" she asked, "You have a hollow leg or something?" Jane glanced down at Butch's long legs in their faded jeans.

"Two," said Butch, as he shoved the last bite of one of the donuts into his mouth. He grinned, as he chewed at Jane, and she thought her heart would burst at how cute he looked with donut glaze all around his mouth.

"Did you get the Sunday paper?" asked Jane, looking over towards the floor where Butch had produced the coffee and donuts.

"No. I forgot. Did you want to read it?"

"Well, I wanted to see if there was anything about Pops' murder or Jennie's disappearance in it."

"Let's not waste our last couple of precious hours thinking about those things," said Butch. He set aside his coffee and suddenly rolled over Jane, forcing her to hold out to her side her coffee with one hand and the donut with the other while Butch kissed her.

"Butch, I'll spill my coffee," she warned as Butch shifted the bed as he began to remove his jeans. He stopped long enough to set Jane's coffee aside.

"I haven't finished my donut," she continued when he had his pants removed and moved under the covers with her. Butch looked annoyed, then proceeded to eat what was left of the donut himself right out from Jane's fingers.

"Oh Butch," said Jane lovingly, as he finished the donut and just before he kissed her. The glaze around his mouth got on hers.

The brief mention of Pops' death and Jennie's disappearance in regards to the Sunday paper was the only one made during their weekend at the LaPierre. A few hours later Butch and Jane packed and checked out and headed for Grangeville, and Jane never told Butch her theory that connected the two. But by Tuesday night Jane would tell Butch, because by then Jennie O'Brien was found.

CHAPTER FIVE

Jane returned to work Monday morning. She had not said a word to any of her fellow deputies, nor to Ralph, where she was going or with whom she was going, but they all knew. Something like going off for a weekend long tryst with someone as well known as Butch wasn't something that could be kept very secretive in a town like Grangeville. But no one in the Sheriff's Department said a word about it. Had it been anyone other than Butch Przybylski who Jane had gone off with, she would have been mercilessly harassed about it by Clark. But Butch and Clark went way back, way back to elementary school in their history, and though he would never admit it Clark was afraid of Butch. Butch always bested Clark in everything, from athletics to being the one to take the cheerleading captain to the senior prom. Clark was simply no match for Butch in the brains department, or any other department for that matter. Yet Clark never hated Butch, he was too scared of him to feel hate. He just treated Butch with a very healthy respect and made sure not to cross him. That was why Clark's hassling of Jane subsided substantially when Jane and Butch began their affair. Clark did not want that famous Przybylski wit and temper coming down on his head.

Ralph, on the other hand, kept silent about it for another reason. Whenever Jane returned from one of these weekends he was even more uncomfortable around her. She had a glow about her that could only come from sexual satisfaction, so much so that almost anyone could sense it. And Ralph did. And he was so disconcerted by the fact Jane had sex he could barely look at her for the first few days she was back. Galen never said anything because he wasn't exactly sure what Jane and Butch did on their long weekends away. He was enough of an innocent to not pick up on Jane's glow and was also too confused as to why Butch and Jane would drive way up state to just stay in a motel room all weekend to be able to figure it out. There was a vague hunch in the back of his mind but he was too embarrassed to ask Clark or Ralph for confirmation.

"Good morning," Jane said, walking into the Sheriff's office and taking off her jacket and setting down the copy of Friday's edition of the Chronicle she had bought that morning on the way in. She was humming a little under her breath as Ralph and Galen looked over at her. Ralph shifted back and forth on his feet uncomfortably and made an uncomfortable grunt in his throat in reply, while Galen looked at her slightly confused before returning her greeting.

"Any news on the O'Brien girl's disappearance Galen?" Jane asked him as she sat down behind her desk.

"Oh, no," said Galen, shaking his head, but more from confusion about Jane than to inform her of the lack of new information. Jane smirked a little as Butch's words regarding Galen's ineptitude about the disappearance returned to her. Her expression was professional but a warm glow appeared in her eyes from the thought of Butch coming into her head. At that moment Ralph chose to look at her full glance and he saw that glow in her eyes. He became so unsettled he turned abruptly and started towards his office.

"Oh, Sheriff, I plan to question Mrs. O'Brien today about her daughter. And some of Jennie's friends. Perhaps what some of them know can offer some clues as to where Jennie might be," said Jane, just before Ralph entered his office. He stopped at the door and only turned his head slightly at her.

"Fine, Deputy. Get right on it," said Ralph. He opened the door quickly and went in, shutting the door swiftly behind him.

Jane looked after Ralph with a somewhat bemused expression on her face. She knew full well what effect her activity with Butch had on Ralph and that it was the reason why he would act this way. She was tempted sometimes to take advantage of it, but her better nature won out and she simply went on as the professional she was.

Now that she was alone with Galen she could ask him a few questions that she couldn't ask Ralph or Clark without arousing suspicion as to why she wanted to know these things. But she started off with a request that would assure Galen was thrown off the tract.

"Could I have the file on the O'Brien girl back, now, Galen?" she asked, picking out a pencil from the holder on the desk.

"Yeah, sure," said Galen. He went to his desk and picked the slim file off it and handed it to Jane.

"Thank you Deputy," she said. She watched from the comer of her eye the way Galen slightly squirmed with pleasure at being called by his title. No one else ever did it. It was always just Galen to everyone else, including the citizens of Grangeville. Jane was the only one who ever called him Deputy. He at least always liked that about her. And it always put him in a receptive mood to do what she asked of him, though he didn't realize it.

"Any news about Pops' autopsy, Deputy?" Jane asked, flipping open the file and going down the top paper with the pencil as a guide.

"Nope, But we did hear from Pops' niece," said Galen.

Jane looked up with slight interest. "Pops' niece?'"

"Yeah. Sylvia Griffiths. The girl whose name the Sheriff found in Pops' address book."

"The Sheriff found," said Jane, with only a slight edge to her voice instead of the heavy one she wanted to use.

"Yeah. He called her Friday, found out she's his niece, his only living relative, and told her about Pops. She said she'd be out here Wednesday for the memorial."

"Memorial?"

"Oh Yeah. You don't know. Some of the people in town are arranging a memorial service for Pops. They're gonna hold it on the high school football field so the whole town can be there."

"I see."

Galen sighed as close to lustily as he would ever get. "I can't wait to see what this Sylvia Griffiths looks like," he said a little dreamily.

"Oh?" asked Jane, curious from hearing such a reaction from little sweet Galen.

"Sheriff said she's a fashion magazine editor in Chicago. You know what those ladies all look like."

"Yes," said Jane slowly, she herself knowing but wondering exactly how small town boy Galen would know such a thing.

Galen sighed again. "I sure hope the Sheriff assigns me to crowd control during the memorial and not traffic so I can get a good look at that Sylvia Griffiths."

"Yes, Deputy," said Jane, amusement an undertone of her voice. If this Sylvia Griffiths was a high fashion knockout as Galen hoped and she suspected, Galen would be absolutely terrified by her and tuck tail and run in the other direction as far from her as he could get.

Jane closed the file and stood.

"I'm going over to Mrs. O'Brien's now, Deputy. I'll be back in about an hour."

"Sure Jane," said Galen misty-eyed, and distractedly. Jane bit at her lower lip to keep from laughing at Galen as she put on her jacket and cap and then left the office.

***

Jane knocked on the O'Brien door. The muffled sound of a vacuum was heard shut off inside and a moment later Mrs. O'Brien came to the door. At the sight of Jane her face brightened.

"You've found Jennie!" she said joyously.

"No Ma'am. I'm afraid we haven't," said Jane.

Mrs. O'Brien's expression changed to one of anger and annoyance.

"Well what is it with you law enforcement people! My daughter's been missing four days!"

"I know," replied Jane. The bemused feeling she had towards Galen disappeared at the agony she heard in the mother's voice. Now she felt only anger towards Galen for being the bumbling, ignorant fool and not doing something towards solving this case. Though Jane then realized if her theory about Jennie' disappearance was true, nothing Galen himself would have thought to do would help her find the girl. "That's why I'm here. I would like to ask you a few background questions that could help give us a breakthrough."

Mrs. O'Brien sighed, then slowly nodded. She stepped back and opened the screen door for Jane.

"Come in," she said.

Jane walked in, removing her cap. The living room was in a slight disarray while a vacuum sat in the middle and a dust rag and furniture polish sat on the coffee table. Mrs. O'Brien scurried past Jane and began to move the vacuum out of the way.

"I wanted the house to be clean. When Jennie comes home," she said.

"Of course," said Jane. Mrs. O'Brien motioned to the chair by the front window.

"Please sit down," she said.

For the first time since she had joined the Grangeville Sheriff's Department Jane found she was receiving no hostile feelings or behavior from a citizen. Mrs. O'Brien didn't seem to notice she was talking to a woman deputy. Yet Jane knew Mrs. O'Brien's preoccupation with Jennie's disappearance had something to do with that. Jane was grateful for this preoccupation for two reasons. First, it kept Mrs. O'Brien from reacting to Jane's weekend away with Butch, and second, Jane could ask some sensitive questions without arousing annoyance or anger in her.

"Mrs. O'Brien, since we haven't found Jennie or a clue as to her whereabouts, I must ask you. Is it possible Jennie doesn't want to be found?" asked Jane, her pen poised above her notepad.

"What do you mean?" asked Mrs. O'Brien, confused and surprised.

"Could Jennie have decided to run away?" asked Jane.

Mrs. O'Brien gasped, then shook her head vehemently.

"No. Never. Jennie had no reason to run away."

"There were no problems at home?" Jane asked carefully.

"No," said Mrs. O'Brien firmly, "We had, have, a good relationship with our daughter. She had no reason to run away from home."

Jane nodded.

"How old is your daughter Mrs. O'Brien?"

"Sixteen."

"She have a lot of friends?"

"Yes. A lot of friends. She is very popular."

"Can you give me a few of their names?"

Mrs. O'Brien thought a moment.

"Sarah Anne Jennings is her best friend," she began, "Megan Willson is another. So is Mary Jo Cummings."

Jane busily wrote their names down.

"They all go to Grangeville High with Jennie?"

"Yes."

"Now how about her boyfriend Steve. How long have he and Jennie been dating?" said Jane.

"About six months. It will be exactly six months on the 24th of this month. They started dating on April 24th and they consider the 24th of every month to be their 'anniversary'."

Mrs. O'Brien smiled fondly as she recalled the behavior. Jane managed a little smile in return though the cutesy behavior turned her stomach.

"So they were going steady."

"Yes."

"You knew of no trouble between them?"

"No. None at all."

"Jennie never confided in you she was unhappy with Steve."

"No. In fact, Jennie said one time they talked of hoping after she graduated from high school the two of them would get married."

Jane made a note of this, this not matching something Steve had said when she questioned him that first night Jennie was missing. She didn't think Mrs. O'Brien realized the discrepancy either, but that too had to come from her preoccupation with Jennie's disappearance.

"How often did Steve and Jennie date?"

"Oh, every night. Except during the school year they will get together to study at the library. But they were together every night whether it was to study or on a date."

"Did they have a curfew?"

"Oh yes. Eleven o'clock on weekends. Ten during the week."

"Did they ever break it?"

"No. Well, maybe once or twice. But not by much. A half hour or so. And they usually called to tell us and the Ballards they were going to be late."

Mrs. O'Brien then gave a small shudder and her poise slipped slightly.

"My daughter's a good girl, Deputy. She wouldn't run away or do anything to deliberately hurt me or her father or her brother. She is a good girl."

Mrs. O'Brien gave a deeper shudder and pressed her balled fist between her eyes, fighting back the tears.

"I believe you, Mrs. O'Brien. And thank you for talking to me." Jane decided it would be unwise and cruel to press Mrs. O'Brien any further. She stood up.

"I'll be leaving now. I promise you we'll let you know the minute we hear anything about your daughter."

"Thank you." Mrs. O'Brien escorted Jane to the door and Jane left.

As Jane replaced her cap and walked to her patrol car parked at the curb, she wished she could have told Mrs. O'Brien not to feel so positive Jennie wouldn't run away. Because if Jennie *didn't* run away and was gone these four days, then foul play had to be suspected. But Jane didn't want to point these out to her, even though Jane suspected foul play from the time she had stood in Pops' bathroom.

Jane went back to the Sheriff's office and transferred her notes from the O'Brien interview to Jennie's file. Next, she read Tim's article in the Chronicle about Jennie's disappearance and added that to the file. Then she began to reconstruct the facts of the girl's disappearance on a separate piece of paper, to be seen by her eyes only.

The office was deserted so Jane had the quiet and privacy to think. First she wrote down that Jennie O'Brien was missing. The last time she was seen was Thursday night, by her boyfriend Steve, in Pebble Creek, but he was not sure exactly where in Pebble Creek. Then she wrote a big why on the paper, and wrote that Steve and Jennie had been there to talk about Jennie wanting to see other boys. Jane then wrote down what Mrs. O'Brien had said, that Jennie was hoping to marry Steve someday. Between the two sentences she put a large question mark. Here was the first discrepancy in the case, the one Mrs. O'Brien hadn't caught. Somebody was lying about Jennie's attitude towards Steve, and Jane's intuition told her it wasn't Mrs. O'Brien.

She added that Jennie had no motive to run away from home, according to Mrs. O'Brien, and again Jane felt she was telling the truth. Jane picked up the paper and studied the words several minutes. All she had was her conjectures that Jennie didn't run away from home, and that she and Steve had not gone up to Pebble Creek to discuss their dating situation. Not much support for her theory that Pops' murder and Jennie's disappearance were linked.

The sound of a door opening brought Jane's attention back from her thoughts and she looked up. Ralph stepped in. He had looked relaxed and comfortable till he caught sight of Jane at her desk, and right before her eyes Jane saw him go thoroughly uptight and nervous.

"Hello Sheriff," she said polity.

"Hello Deputy," Ralph replied. As he started heading quickly to his office the telephone on Jane's desk rang.

"Grangeville Sheriff's Department," she said, picking it up. She listened a few moments, then held the receiver out towards Ralph. "It's for you, Sheriff."

Ralph stopped and fidgeted in his spot a moment, then walked over to Jane. When he took the receiver his fingers slightly brushed hers. He went red as he placed the phone to his face.

"Sheriff Parsons," he said.

Jane looked at Ralph as he listened. The embarrassment in his face lessened as he became involved in the conversation on the other end. He was on the line only for about a minute.

"Thank you for calling. Yes, I appreciate it. Goodbye." And Ralph hung up Jane's phone.

"What was that about, Sheriff?" asked Jane.

Ralph's regained poise slipped only a little as he spoke to Jane.

'That was an update on the Griffiths' crime scene. They found two blood types, Type O, which was Pops', and Type B. Which had to have been the murderer's."

"Are they sure about that?" asked Jane.

Ralph scowled at Jane, his embarrassment of her completely vanished now.

"Who else's could it be, Deputy?"

Jane pursed her lips a moment. "Anything else in the report, Sheriff?" she added.

"And they found two sets of fingerprints on the murder weapon, Pops', and an unknown set"

"The murderer's," said Jane.

Ralph scowled again. Now Jane was thinking these were the murderer's, but she didn't think the blood was?

"Yes," agreed Ralph. He started for his office again, this time calmly and with ease. But Jane's voice stopped him halfway there.

"Wasn't there *anything* else in the report Sheriff? Anything unusual about the blood?"

"Like what, Deputy?"

Jane tapped the fingers on her left hand on her desk impatiently.

"It was just blood? Just Type B blood? There wasn't anything else to it?"

"You mean like drugs?" asked Ralph.

"Like, anything else," said Jane, frustrated.

Ralph shook his head. "Nothing else. It was Type B blood and nothing else," he said.

He reached his door and Jane stopped him again.

"I would like to go question some of Jennie's friends at the high school now, Sheriff," she said to him across the room.

"Fine, Deputy. Do that," said Ralph. Annoyance had thoroughly dissolved his embarrassment of Jane now and his tone was brisk. He walked into his office but heard the outside door open and close as Jane left.

***

Grangeville Senior High School sprawled out over several acres two miles from downtown Grangeville. The building housing the auditorium was a huge, tan brick structure, the largest part of the school, with, in proud school colors of blue and white, in block letters, "Grangeville Senior High" tacked on the broad wall. Like a long arm bent at the elbow an offshoot of the auditorium building swung around the grassy courtyard in front of it. Here the classrooms were located. On the other side of the auditorium was the football field, with the bleachers, scoreboard and high wire fence surrounding it. It was a clean, neat, solid building where, Grangeville boasted, clean, neat, solid kids attended. All the students who wanted to go were admitted quickly into the college of their choice, and all the sports teams were always in the thick of the championship races. Grangeville Senior High was the crown jewel in the Grangeville tiara.

Jane's patrol car pulled up in the circular drive in front of the courtyard and parked in front of the auditorium building. Two teenage boys stood outside of it by the six large glass door entrances and were immediately alert at the sight of the car, and were more so when they saw it was Jane who emerged. They were smirking obnoxiously as Jane walked up towards the doors.

"Howdy Deputy," the taller of the two said smartly, causing the other one to snicker under his breath. "You here to arrest sumbody?" he added in a tone that sounded like he didn't believe Jane had the nerve to do such a thing. The second one snickered again, but louder. Jane sighed. These kids didn't look more than sixteen, and already they were smart aleck male chauvinist pigs.

"No. Though I might arrest you two for truancy. Why aren't you in class?" asked Jane calmly but firmly.

"We got permission to be here. We're goin' with Mr. Lange to Evans Lumberyard to pick up some more lumber for wood shop," said the taller one, now smugly, "We're just waitin' for him to come around with his pickup."

"What are your names?" asked Jane.

"Randy Monaghan," said the taller one.

"Walter Terry," said the shorter one.

"Well, all right Walter. Randy. I'll take your word on this," said Jane. She eyed the two. "But in case you're really interested, I'm here to ask some questions about Jennie O'Brien. You two know anything about her being missing?"

The two boys' expressions changed as swiftly and abruptly as the sun going behind a sudden dark cloud. They suddenly went from self-assured cocky to a silent, heavy stun. Walter glanced downward and studied his battered tennis shoes. Randy suddenly found it urgent to look out over the driveway for his wood shop teacher.

"Well, do you?" said Jane strongly. Still they didn't answer. "I guess you two aren't as smart as you led me on to believe," she added, now the self-confident one.

She now smiled brashly and started towards the door again. But Randy suddenly recovered his voice.

"We don't know nuthin' about Jenne O'Brien or where she is," he stated boldly.

Jane turned and looked at them, Walter still engrossed with his sneakers.

"That's all I wanted to know," she said, then continued into the school.

Jane might have basked in her little victory over the young male bias except their reactions she found more important. She saw the change in their attitude when Jennie O'Brien was mentioned, so knew that they actually did know something about her disappearance. But she felt she would get more from the three girls Mrs. O'Brien had said were Jennie's closest friends, so she left the boys standing there and walked up the stairs to the main hallway of the school. But Jane made a mental note of the two boys' names.

Jane walked down the deserted corridor, classes being in session, past the rooms, some of which had their doors open. The hallway was so quiet the handcuffs clinking against Jane's belt echoed loudly, and caught the attention of the students sitting closest to the classroom door. As Jane walked by the students noticed her, then whispered excitedly to the student sitting nearby.

Jane came to the principal's office and walked in. The principal's secretary, Mrs. Alice French, Andy's mother, sat behind her desk typing. She looked up when Jane entered and registered surprise. Mrs. French did not like Jane being a Sheriff's deputy anymore than the next person in town, but she handled it differently. She kept trying to convince Jane to do something else. Like, after Jane started going with Butch, marry Butch and have lots of nice babies.

"Can I help you Deputy?" she asked, removing her glasses and letting them hang from the chain that circled her neck and was attached to the frame. Someone could tell Mrs. French was Andy's mother, they looked very much alike, same longish oval face, long nose, tiny mouth and somewhat unkempt brown hair, Andy's almost as long as his mothers, except Mrs. French wore hers pinned up.

"I need to speak to a few of your students, Mrs. French," said Jane, Would you get them out of class for me. I won't keep them long, I just have a few questions about Jennie O'Brien I'd like to ask them."

Mrs. French's expression began to look very reluctant to Jane's request, till the mention of Jennie O'Brien. Then it went dead serious and she stood up.

"Let me get Principal Ross," she said

Alice French tapped on the frosted pane of glass of the door behind her desk and walked in. On the glass was painted in black block letters

"Henry Ross, Principal." A few seconds later the door opened again. Mrs. French nodded inwards.

"Principal Ross will talk to you," she said.

It was on the tip of Jane's tongue to say Principal Ross wasn't who she wanted to talk to, but she held tack and walked past Mrs. French into the office.

Henry Ross was a short, powerfully built man, always looking as if he was stuffed into the three-piece suits he always wore in school. Butch said it was because he was too cheap to buy new ones that fit better and too disinclined to lose weight. Butch also added he remembered the suits Henry wore these days back when he, Butch, went to Grangeville High twenty years ago. Henry had a full face that hung in flabs around his neck and jowls. His hair was pure white and very thin. The only thing he possessed that was a usual sign of warmth and friendliness was his blue eyes, but warm and friendly Henry Ross was not. He was a good principal, and fair, as long as a student toed the line Henry drew, but to those natural rebels of the teen set, he was the devil incarnate. And the most notorious of those rebels in the history of Grangeville High was Butch Przybylski, who had run-ins with Principal Ross practically every week of the four years he attended the school. It was only Butch's excellent academic record and prowess on the athletic fields that kept him from being suspended from school so many times. It didn't matter that Butch was Principal Ross's only nephew.

It was this love-hate relationship towards Butch that Jane felt she was up against with Henry, since he knew Jane was having an affair with Butch, and didn't approve of the extent it went. This plus not liking Jane being a deputy built up quite a barrier Jane knew she would have to deal with in talking with Henry. Principal Ross was sitting back in his swivel chair as Jane came in, his fingers laced together resting on his considerable girth.

"Deputy," Henry said contemptuously. Jane was expecting contempt and she was ready for it.

"Principal Ross. I'll get right to the point as to why I'm here. I would like to talk to three of your students regarding the disappearance of Jennie O'Brien," Jane said firmly, looking Henry right in the eye.

"Oh, you would, would you?" said Henry, slightly sarcastically.

"Yes sir. The students are three of Jennie's friends. Sarah Jennings, Megan Willson and Mary Jo Cummings."

"I see," said Henry. He sat forward in his chair and looked at a paper on his desk. "Well, all three girls will be in third hour." Henry then sat back again. "This would mean interrupting their class."

"Mr. Ross, we are talking about a young woman's life here," snapped Jane, "Now there's no question Jennie's well-being is more important than these girls' classes." Jane rested her hands on Henry's desk and leaned in towards him. "Now you can let me see these girls right now, or I'll go get three subpoenas and drag them out of class later. Which is it?"

Henry Ross gave a small sly smile, but in his eyes Jane saw a glint of fear. He blinked a few times and it disappeared, but then a moment later so did the sly smile. He teed forward again and picked up a sheet of paper from his desk.

"I thought someone might come to question them. So I had Mrs. French pull their schedules. Sarah and Mary Jo are in Home Ec. Megan is in English class."

Jane stood back up slowly.

"Thank you," she said solemnly.

"I'll go get them now," said Henry, rising with some difficulty.

"I would like some place private to talk to them," added Jane.

"You can use my office," said Henry, before he left.

Jane folded her arms and sat on the edge of Henry's desk, fuming. So Henry had planned on someone talking to the three girls all along, and had the necessary information right before him even before she came in. But he was still biased enough against her to actually, deliberately, give her a hard time about seeing the girls even though another one was missing. Was everyone's hatred against her as a deputy that strong that it even overwhelmed their concern for a missing girl? Jane had hoped the seriousness of her investigation would make people put aside their prejudices and treat her as any law enforcement officer on this important case. But obviously not even a situation as serious as this did it completely. Jane's anger cooled a little when she realized at the bottom line it didn't matter if Henry was driven to play his little difficulty game with her. It wasn't going to matter to Jennie's recovery one way or the other.

Jane was sitting behind Henry's desk when the door opened again five mines later and Jennie's three girlfriends walked in. They were all Jennie's type; pretty, fresh-faced, carefully groomed and dressed. Megan Willson was the shortest, a petite little thing with long red hair and blue eyes. Sarah Anne Jennings was the tallest, a willowy brunette with icy green eyes. Mary Jo Cummings was the typical cheerleader type. Long golden blonde hair, blue eyes, beautiful face and dressed in the uniform of the Grangeville Senior High cheerleader.

"Girls, this is Deputy Fleming," said Henry, "She would like to talk to you a few minutes."

Henry shut the door behind them, and the girls, clustered together, walked up to the desk nervously. Jane eyed them as they stood before her like three frightened kittens.

"As Principal Ross said, I'm Deputy Fleming. But you can call me Jane," she said.

Jane smiled, but instead of putting the girls at ease even a little, they shifted on their feet and glanced around the room with their eyes. Their activities made Jane realize these girls would be able to tell her a lot about Jennie O'Brien, if she could just get it all out of them.

"Would you like to sit down? Are there chairs for each of you?" asked Jane, looking around the room.

" We'll stand," said Sarah, but Mary Jo went to the one lone chair against the wall by Henry's desk and sat.

"Now I know your names, but who is who, here?" asked Jane, as she took out her pen and notepad and flipped it open.

"I'm Megan," said the little redhead, "This is Sarah." She indicated her with a motion of her hand. "And this is Mary Jo."

Jane nodded. "Well, girls, I think you know why I asked Principal Ross to bring you here. Mrs. O'Brien told me you are Jennie's closest friends."

"We don't know anything about Jennie being missing," said Mary Jo suddenly from the chair by the wall.

"All right," said Jane. She mentally noted Mary Jo's sudden belligerency and sharp tone, "That's one question I was going to ask you. But there are others. I hope you'll be able to answer them, truthfully."

"What do you want to know?" asked Sarah, who appeared to be the most together of the three nervous girls.

"First, I need to know if Jennie told you why she and Steve were going up to Pebble Creek on their last date."

"They went up to Pebble Creek?" asked Megan, surprised.

"Shut up Megan!" snapped Mary Jo sharply.

Megan turned her head swiftly to look at Mary Jo. And Jane studied the reaction going on between them.

"You thought they were going somewhere else, Megan?" Jane asked.

"No," said Megan, turning her head back around, only now looking down at the floor.

Jane studied Megan a few moments till Mary Jo spoke up sharply.

"Jennie and Steve went up to Pebble Creek for the same reason everybody else does. To make out," said Mary Jo strongly.

"Did Jennie tell you this?" asked Jane.

Mary Jo shifted in her chair, more confident now, sitting up straighter.

"They went there every date. She and Steve had their own special make-out spot up there. A spot off of the big bend in the road just past the parking area. They could see all of the town from up there."

"But this last time, did she tell you they were going up there for any particular reason?" asked Jane.

"No," Mary Jo.

"Are you girls pretty close to Jennie?"

"Yes," said Sarah.

"Would she have told you she was going up to Pebble Creek for any other reason than to make out?" asked Jane.

"Of course she would. She's our best friend," piped up Megan, "We tell each other everything…"

"Did she ever tell you she wanted to date other guys?" inquired Jane.

"Oh no," said Sarah, "Jennie didn't want to date other guys. She loved Steve. She wasn't interested in anyone else."

Jane nodded and jotted the answers down in her notepad. Here was her hunch about Mrs. O'Brien's being the one who was correct about Steve and Jennie's relationship verified. So now she was sure Steve was lying when he said he and Jennie went up to Pebble Creek to talk about Jennie wanting to date other guys. And there was certainly no fight about it where Jennie went running off. And he was lying about not knowing where they were, exactly.

"Did Jennie ever tell you she was unhappy at home?" continued Jane.

The three girls looked at each other in what Jane saw was completely sincere guess. So when they all replied in the negative, she believed them. She now completely dismissed the theory that Jennie had run away, even though she had never given it any credence in the first place.

"Now I'd like to know, from each of you, what do *you* think happened to Jennie?" asked Jane.

Jane looked squarely at each girl as they immediately clamed up. Little Megan also went beet red and looked at the floor again. Sarah drifted on her feet and chewed her lower lip. And Mary Jo's jaw visibly clamped tighter.

"Well?" said Jane.

Still the girls remained silent.

"She's your best friend. What do you think has happened to her?"

The girls continued to be silent. The longer they did the more sure Jane was that they knew what had happened to Jennie, or at least knew the something that could lead to finding out what happened to her.

"You told me that Jennie didn't want to date anybody else," said Jane, "But Steve told me he and Jennie went up to Pebble Creek to talk about Jennie wanting to date other boys. And when they got into a fight about it Jennie ran off. That's how she disappeared, according to Steve. Now somebody's lying, or you three aren't as good friends with Jennie as you believe."

The girls now exchanged looks of surprise, but still said nothing. Jane's patience began to wear thin.

"Why don't one of you just break down and tell me what happened to Jennie," she said firmly and slightly sharply, "You'll feel better and you'll save the O'Briens a lot of misery and anguish. Tell me."

But still, the three girls remained speechless. Jane noticed it looked for a split second Megan was going to speak, but an incredibly intimidating look from Mary Jo stopped her. Jane pressed her lips together and stood, flipping shut her notepad and putting it away along with her pen.

"All right. You each know where you can reach me. If you feel like finally talking to me."

Jane walked around Principal Ross's desk and to the door. But suddenly she stopped when Mary Jo spoke.

"What do *you* think happened to Jennie, Deputy?" she asked smartly.

Turning to her, Jane's gaze bore into Mary Jo so hard all the confidence Mary Jo had built up before wilted down to nothing.

"I think Jennie got herself into a lot of trouble," she said.

Jane opened the door and took a step out. But then she stopped again, and leaned back into the room.

"Oh yes, I do have one more question.

The three girls looked up and over to Jane in unison.

"Did Jennie ever do any business at Pops' store?"

The look in the three girls' eyes were enough for Jane, and she stopped outside of the room, shutting the door behind her.

Principal Ross and Mrs. French were waiting in the outer office when Jane emerged. They both looked up at her when she did.

"You can send the girls back to their classes now, Mr. Ross," said Jane.

"Did they tell you everything you wanted to know?" asked Mrs. French.

"No," said Jane, "But one of them probably will, eventually." Jane went to the outer door now but stopped again.

"Oh yes, I would like to speak to the school nurse," she said, "Where is her office?"

"I'll take you there," said Mrs. French, standing.

As she and Jane walked down the hall the bell rang and third hour was over. Students came pouring out of the rooms and began streaming through the corridors around them. Most of them paid no attention to Mrs. French but hurried on their way to their next class. The rest greeted Mrs. French warmly. But all of them shot either dirty, inquisitive or a combination of both glances at Jane. Finally she and Mrs. French passed the school trophy case, turned the corner and reached the nurse's station, just as the hall cleared and the second attendance bell rang.

"Thank you for bringing me here, Mrs. French," said Jane, "Say hello to Andy for me when you see him," she added, hoping to sound conclusive and turning quickly to the door before Alice could say more. But she wasn't quick enough.

"And how is Butch doing?" Alice asked sweetly.

Jane could only stop and nod quickly.

"He's fine."

"You say hello to him for me too, won't you? He's a good man, Butch. Oh, he has some rough edges, but basically he'd make any girl a good husband. You keep that in mind, now, Janie girl. Guys like Butch don't grow on trees. You grab him before he's snapped up by some other girl."

"Yes Mrs. French," said Jane. She returned a weak smile to Mrs. French's broad one before going into the nurse's office.

The room appeared to be empty when Jane walked in. It was equipped for medical emergencies, with gurneys and supplies in cabinets which lined the walls. Jane didn't know who the school nurse was, but a desk next to the door caught Jane's eye and saw the nameplate on it. The name stamped on it was "Miss Annabell Cromie."

"Nurse Cromie?" she called out.

In the back of her mind Jane expected anyone named Annabell to be a petite, gentle-looking little woman. Who responded to her call was no petite, gentle-looking little woman. From a door far in the back wall came a tall, tough-looking Amazon of a woman, in her early fifties, with heavily grayed brown hair pulled back in a sever bun and piercing little eyes squinting out from the plump folds of her face. She came stomping down towards Jane in a tight-fitting white nurse's uniform and cap. Nurse Cromie took Jane in with one swift glance, and Jane saw immediately an antagonistic look come into her beady eyes.

"I'm Nurse Cromie," she said in a husky voice.

"Nurse Cromie, I'm Deputy Fleming. I'm investigating the disappearance of one of the students, Jennie O'Brien."

Now Jane saw a struggle begin within Nurse Cromie, a struggle between her dislike of Jane the female deputy and the need to find the O'Brien girl. As she stared at Jane there appeared to be no settlement of the struggle.

"What can I do for you?" she asked.

"I would like to see Jennie O'Brien's file," Jane said.

Now an outcome appeared to be happening in Nurse Cromie's struggle, and she scowled slightly.

"What do you want to see that for?" asked Nurse Cromie.

"I need to find some information that could lead to the recovery of the girl," said Jane.

Nurse Cromie shook her head, now firmly decided against Jane.

"Those files are confidential," she said, "I can't allow you to see it."

"Nurse Cromie, considering the circumstances I think we can disregard that rule," insisted Jane.

"What possible information can be in her file that would help you find her?" asked Nurse Cromie impatiently.

"I just need to learn one bit of information that will confirm something about Jennie I need to know," said Jane.

"And what's that?" demanded Nurse Cromie.

Jane didn't want to get that deep with the school nurse, she just wanted to come in, check what she needed to know and get out, without drawing anyone else into her search. But it didn't look like Nurse Cromie was going to let her do this. Jane sighed and placed her hands on her holster, standing arms akimbo.

"I'd like to learn Jennie's blood type," she said.

"I don't see what her blood type has to do with finding her," said Nurse Cromie. She shook her head firmly. "No. You can't see her file."

"Nurse Cromie, I can go get a subpoena and force you to show it to me. Eventually I will see that file. Why postpone the inevitable?"

"Because until I have to, I'm not showing you that file," stated Nurse Cromie belligerently, "Now I want you to leave. I have things to do."

She actually grabbed Jane's arm and pulled her around and lead her to the door. Opening it, she firmly pushed Jane out and shut it with a heavy thud.

Jane stood a few moments in shock at actually being manhandled by Nurse Cromie. But there were few people who could deter Jane when she had her mind set on doing something, and Nurse Cromie wasn't one of them. Jane's shock wore off quickly and her mind quickly formulated an idea. All she had to do was wait another hour and the first lunch period, and pick out two kids she would get to help her.

***

The cafeteria was filled with noisy students when Jane walked in. None of them paid her any attention as she stood off to the side looking them over. Her glance stopped when she saw Randy and Walter sitting at the end of one of the long tables eating their sack lunches.

"Hi fellas," she said, walking up to them and standing at the end of the table.

"Hello Deputy," said Randy, while chewing a large bite of bologna sandwich robustly. Walter looked at Jane carefully as he chewed on a peanut butter and jelly sandwich. "What do you want?"

"How would you guys like to help me out on a little police work?" asked Jane carefully. But Randy and Walter sat away from the rest of the students, and the noise level continued being high, so no one overheard her.

"Police work?" said Walter eagerly. His face lit up as Jane often saw Pete's did when she talked of Sheriff Department matters. Jane knew right there she had Walter sewn up for her little plan. But Randy was still unconverted towards Jane.

"We ain't interested," he said. He grabbed his carton of milk and took a long draw on his straw.

"There's ten dollars in it. For each of you," said Jane.

At the mention of money Walter's face lit up even more. Randy froze in mid-slurp and looked up at Jane.

"What do you say fellas?" asked Jane.

Walter and Randy looked at each other, Randy still frozen in mid-slurp. When he did nothing else Walter grinned and looked up at Jane.

"What do we have to do?" he asked.

Jane leaned down and set her forearms on the table between Walter and Randy, so her head was even with theirs.

"I want you to get Nurse Cromie out of her office and keep her out for about five minutes. Think you can do it?" she asked.

Walter sat back in his chair and a confident smirk appeared on his face.

"Piece of cake," he said. Then his smirk got deeper. "But gee, pullin' one over on of Horse-face Cromie is worth it anyway. Who needs to be paid?"

Randy finally swallowed and took the straw out of his mouth while giving Walter a good swift kick under the table for his last words. Walter let out a yelp of pain. Jane looked amused.

"Good. Then as soon as you fellas are done with your lunch, meet me in the hallway next to the trophy case."

"Just a minute," said Randy, regaining his voice. He looked stern. "We get paid up front."

Jane straightened and looked down at the slick little dealer, and pursed her lips. Then she reached into her hip pocket and drew out her wallet. Opening it, she picked out two bills and slapped one down in front of each.

"Five now. Five after the job is done. Successfully," she said.

Jane stood next to the trophy case, her back to the wall. From around the corner she could hear Randy's footsteps walking towards the nurse's office. She heard the door open and Randy go in. There was several moments of silence, then the door opened again and she heard two voices.

"But he can't come here, Nurse Cromie. He's awfully sick. He can't even get out of the boys' john. Walter said the cramps in his stomach's so bad, he can't walk," came Randy's voice.

"Well all right. I'll go take a look at him. Which boys' room did you say he was in?" came Nurse Cromie's.

"The one all the way down by the gym."

As Jane listened the sound of their footsteps slowly faded down the hall in the opposite direction and disappeared. Then quickly she turned the corner and silently sprinted down the hall to the door of the nurse's station.

Quietly Jane opened the door and slipped in. There was no sign of any files in the outer room, so Jane headed for the one she originally saw Nurse Cromie come out of. She opened this door and was greeted with the sight of two large metal file cabinets against the wall to her left.

The drawers were labeled with the alphabet and she slid open the one marked M thru P. Fortunately for Jane, Nurse Cromie was an efficient filer and Jane had no trouble finding the Os and Jennie O'Brien's file. Drawing it out Jane opened it and started to read.

There wasn't much to it, just Jennie's basic health history and a few notes on the two times she had seen Nurse Cromie. Jane scanned the paper quickly and began to fear she wasn't going to find what she was looking for. But printed on the inside back of the file was a chart, and on it was what Jane needed to know. Jennie O'Brien's blood type.

CHAPTER SIX

Lunchtime found Jane driving the patrol car home to eat. Butch's Mustang was already in the driveway and she parked behind it. They were eating lunch at home today, and Butch was preparing it.

Jane rafted in she was going on her lunch break after her escapade in the high school. She had waited in the patrol car for Randy and Walter to show up so she could pay them the rest of their money. Fifteen minutes after Jane returned to her car they arrived. Walter had an unhappy look on his face.

"You did great, guys, thanks," said Jane, as she handed them each five dollars.

"It didn't *feel* so great," said Walter, 'That ol' battle ax nurse dosed me with some gosh-awful stuff." He stuck out his tongue. "Uck! I can still taste it."

Jane smiled sympathetically.

"Sorry you had to endure that Walter. Here." Jane brought out another five dollar bill. "For action above and beyond the call of duty."

"Gee, thanks!" said Walter, his face lighting up again and all signs of distaste leaving his face. Randy eyed the extra money longingly but said nothing.

"Better get back in school, guys. And thanks again," said Jane, starting the car.

"You're welcome Deputy," said Walter. The way he was looking at her Jane knew she had a friend for life now in Walter Terry. Suddenly Randy spoke up.

"Hey Deputy," he said. Jane hit the brake and put the car back in neutral and looked at him. "Just why did you have us do this? Why did you want to get into the nurse's office alone?"

"Had to check on something, Randy, that Nurse Cromie didn't want to show me."

"What's that?" asked Randy.

"Jennie O'Brien's medical file," said Jane.

As before the two boys' expressions changed swiftly to uncomfortable ones. Jane looked at them closely.

"What did you have to find in Jennie's medical file?" asked Walter.

"Her blood type," said Jane, continuing to watch them carefully.

The two boys looked at each other this time, and Jane saw a little of actual horror now in their expressions. These kids did know something, if she could just get them to tell her.

"Guys, if you know something, anything, about Jennie O'Brien, please tell me. Look, you've helped me to look at her medical file, so you're involved in this investigation now. Tell me what you know so I'll know too!"

Jane looked at them earnestly, but neither boy could look at her squarely now. She waited a moment but it was soon obvious they weren't going to say anything, anymore than Jennie's three girlfriends were going to tell everything they knew. Jane sighed and put the car in gear again. She was only a split second away from driving off when Randy spoke.

"This wasn't suppose to happen, Deputy," he said, as Jane hit the brake hard and looked up at him. "Nothing was supposed to happen to Jennie. She wasn't supposed to disappear or anything. She and Steve were just going to..." Randy stopped and then hit Walter on the arm and motioned him to follow. Randy walked off and Walter did too. Jane watched them leave and disappear into the school. A deep sigh emitted from her, as she was sure if Randy finished his sentence, he would have confirmed for her, without a doubt, that what she had theorized in the beginning about Jennie O'Brien was absolutely, positively, true.

She heard Butch moving around in the kitchen when she came into the house. She removed her hat and jacket and holster and set them on one of the chairs. Jesse came from the kitchen and demanded attention and Jane scratched his ears and patted him.

"Butch?" she called out, "I'm here."

Jesse followed her as she walked into the kitchen and found Butch standing at the counter chopping up a long stalk of celery with a large butcher knife somewhat viciously. The small table in the breakfast nook by the big bay window in the kitchen was appealingly set with a very appetizing lunch. But the scowl on Butch's face was what Jane noticed more.

"Butch?" she repeated.

He looked up but the scowl did not disappear when he saw Jane. A little lump caught in her throat as she took that scowl to mean he was mad at her. But what could he be mad at her about? She wasn't late for lunch.

"What's the matter Butch?" she asked, swallowing the lump in her throat to speak.

"I got word this morning that the softball tournament games tonight might be canceled!" he said between clenched teeth.

"What?" said Jane, surprised, and also relieved that this was what Butch was upset about. "Why?"

"Because of that old Billy goat's death," said Butch. He started in on the celery stalk again, bits of it flying off around the counter and on the floor.

"You mean Pops Griffiths'?" asked Jane.

"Yeah," said Butch. He finished with the stalk of celery before him and reached over and started on another.

"Oh, I'm sorry Butch," she said, "Did whoever told you say when they might be rescheduled?

Butch stopped chopping and looked at the quite large pile he had on the chopping board.

"Well, they're not exactly canceled." He looked up at Jane and the scowl was gone. 'The word was the officials were *thinking* about canceling them. But we're still all supposed to show up at Huber Field to play. They'll let us know then.

"They should let you play. Things have to go on as normal," said Jane.

"My thoughts exactly," he said. Good humor returned to him and he smiled at Jane. Then he walked over to her, grabbed her head and kissed her enthusiastically. "Two great minds with but a single thought," he said when he released the kiss and her head. "Let's eat. I'm starved."

"So am I," said Jane. Butch escorted her to the table and helped her gallantly into her chair. Jane took her napkin and set it on her lap as she looked over the table.

"Everything looks so good, Butch," she said, as he went around to the other side of the table and sat opposite her. Jesse sat nearby, ready for any tidbit Jane or Butch might offer him.

"Well, my mother taught me the way to a woman's heart is through her stomach," said Butch. Then he grinned. "Then I found out myself a nice-looking table is the quickest way into her pants. Dig in," he added, and proceeded to do so with the macaroni salad in the bowl on the table.

"Did you hear about the memorial this Wednesday too? asked Jane, biting into the thick tuna fish sandwich.

"No. What memorial?" asked Butch, pouring himself and Jane some Pepsi from a bottle into their glasses filled with ice.

"Galen told me about it this morning. Some townspeople are arranging a service for Pops on the high school football field."

Butch made a sound of disgust in his throat as he chewed a carrot. "This town is out of it's collective mind," he said after swallowing.

"I guess the town shouldn't expect you to be there then," said Jane with a small smile.

"Hell no. Are you going to have to be there?"

"Yes. I'll have to be there before for crowd control or directing traffic."

"And during?" Butch asked, then crunching a potato chip and offering one to Jesse. He eagerly came forward and noisily chewed it.

"Well, I'll have to stay to direct the crowd or traffic afterwards."

Butch grunted unhappily. "Oh. I thought you could come back to town while everyone's away and we could make love in the middle of Main Street."

"Aren't you curious to see Pops' niece?" Jane asked.

"Pops' niece?" said Butch, puzzled.

Jane explained how she found the woman's name in Pops' address book, and when contacted, said she was Pops' only living relative and would be there Wednesday from Chicago. Butch only barely nodded to the information as he devoted most of his attention to his lunch. His interest only became strong when Jane mentioned how Ralph took credit for finding the address himself.

"Why that son-of-a-bitch," Butch snapped.

"I saw your Uncle Henry this afternoon," said Jane, helping herself to more macaroni salad.

"Oh? And what did you have to see *that* son-of-a-bitch for?" asked Butch. But before Jane could answer the phone rang. Butch excused himself and got up to answer it.

"Hello?" he said. Then a moment later his face broke into a wide grin. "All right," he said, punching the air with his fist. He listened a few seconds more as Jane turned in her chair to look at him. Then he said good-bye and hung up the receiver.

"What is it Butch?" asked Jane, turning her body to follow his trip back to his chair.

"That was Andy. The softball game's on tonight!" said Butch happily, sitting back down.

"Oh good," said Jane in relief.

"Yeah, the Przybylski Garage Pit Bulls will again reign supreme tonight and retain their Cass County Amateur Softball League Championship."

"I forgot. Who do you play tonight?" asked Jane.

"The winner of the Wheeler's Bar and Grill Marauders from Marcellus and the Van Lacken Tool & Die Indians from Pokagan game, which is the first game. Then there's some kind of 'half-time' show and then the Pit Bulls play."

Butch finished his lunch and pushed back his plate.

"Want some dessert?" he asked, before finishing up his Pepsi.

Jane shook her head swiftly. "Can't eat another bite, Butch. I'm full."

Butch narrowed his eyes.

"I wasn't talking about any dessert to eat," he said.

Jane's look met Butch's evenly, then she glanced at her watch.

"We do have forty minutes," she said, fixing her look with his again.

"Then let's go," said Butch. He stood up and went over to Jane and took her hand. She stood too and began to follow him to the bedroom. Jesse saw where they were going and knew not to follow, he laid down in the kitchen and sighed deeply.

"Butch," Jane said as they walked down the hallway.

"Is this a good idea when you've got this big softball game tonight?"

Butch stood and thought a moment.

"Yes," he said simply, then continued into the bedroom with Jane.

Jane returned to the Sheriff's office after lunch and "dessert" with Butch. Ralph and Galen were there when she came in, and the glow she always had after making love with Butch was twice as noticeable now as when she came back after a weekend with him. Her demeanor was as always professional, but the look in her eyes made it so obvious what she had been doing with Butch, besides eating lunch, during her lunch hour it could not be denied. At least to Ralph. When he saw her come in fresh from Butch's bed, he practically became apoplectic with discomfort. Ever innocent little Galen however only saw Jane appeared to be in a good mood.

"Hi Jane," he said sprightly, "Have a good lunch?"

The papers in Ralph's hand rattled slightly at Galen's question. Jane eyed Ralph knowingly and amused while answering Galen.

"It was magnificent, Galen," she said enthusiastically.

"Wow. That must have been some lunch Butch made her," said Galen under his breath to Ralph. Ralph went absolutely beet red at the comment while Jane continued to watch him, now even more amused. And it didn't help Ralph's composure when Jane spoke to him.

"I'd like to go over my notes on Mrs. O'Brien's and Jennie's friends' interviews with you Sheriff," Jane said, utterly professional. Ralph couldn't speak and only made grunts in his throat. "When you have time," she added.

Ralph made a sound in his throat that sounded like "Uh huh," and started for his office door yet again quickly. He was stopped when the phone on the front desk rang and Jane went to answer it.

"Grangeville Sheriff's Department," she said into the phone.

Ralph's embarrassment dimmed a little as he and Galen watched the expression on Jane's face change.

"Give me your address," she said, picking up a pencil and holding it poised above a notepad on the desk. She scribbled something down. "Someone will be right there Ma'am. Good-bye."

Ralph now regained his composure, and Galen looked on with curiosity as Jane tossed down the pencil and ripped off the notepad sheet with the address on it.

"That was a Mrs. Robbins, Sheriff. She said her husband is in trouble. She was too upset to explain how, exactly. Her address is 1116 Shady Lane."

"I know it. Let's get going," said Ralph. He reached into his office and pulled out his jacket. Jane and Galen both stood, not sure if he meant either one or both of them. Ralph immediately saw their confusion.

"Deputy, you took the call, you come with me. Galen, you stay here," said Ralph.

Jane and Ralph hurried out while Galen remained behind and brooded a little at Jane being referred to as Deputy while he was Galen.

Shady Lane was out west of Pebble Creek in the more rural section of Grangeville. Jane and Ralph drove their patrol cars down the road with both sirens and flashers going. They turned into the driveway of 1116 Shady Lane and before they even stopped, an older, heavyset woman came lumbering around the corner of the house from the back as fast as her fat, short legs could carry her.

"Oh help, help! It's my husband! Please help him!" she wailed.

Both Jane and Ralph were out of their cars in a second and started running around the house in the direction the woman had come from. But Ralph was not all that smaller than the woman and only ran barely faster than she did. Jane sped out way in front of him even though she had started out behind Ralph. Ralph saw Jane reach the rear of the house and turn, then suddenly stop and freeze in position, staring down at the house. Ralph lumbered up next to Jane and stopped in start too, and stared.

There in a narrow basement window was a large, older man wedged between the window frame. He was caught on his stomach, his head, shoulders and chest on the outside and the rest of him on the inside. He was struggling frustratingly when Jane came up but when he saw her, he stopped and looked at her sheepishly. Ralph came up then and the man's expression became even more embarrassed.

"Dang it Ralph" he said, "I told Edna not to call you."

Ralph held a snicker back but not very well. Jane now looked relieved that it was not a life-threatening situation and smiled a little to herself too. She wanted to burst out laughing but knew it wasn't the professional thing to do.

"So George, how in the hell did you get yourself in this situation?" asked Ralph, coming over and squatting next to George.

"Oh, I was painting the basement stairs, and Edna called me for lunch. I couldn't come up the stairs because like a dang fool I went and painted the wrong way, I painted myself down into the basement. But I thought I could get out through this window." George looked to each side. "Guess my stomach's bigger than my eyes."

"Well, I'd better call the fire department on this," said Ralph. He looked the window and George over. "Doesn't look like there's anything we can do."

"Oh, for Christ's sake Ralph. Don't bring the fire department in on this too!" said George disgustedly. But Ralph only grinned and stood up. Edna waddled up then from around the house, and came up to Ralph, grabbing his arm.

"Ralph, can you help him!" Edna wailed.

"No Edna, we're going to need the fire department to get George out of this. Can I use your phone?"

"Yes."

Edna led Ralph to the back door and they both disappeared into the house, leaving Jane and George alone outside. George eyed Jane critically but kindly.

"I suppose you're getting a real kick out of this young woman," he said.

"Not particularly sir," said Jane.

"Don't lie to me. I know you're laughing your head off inside."

Jane finally grinned fully and nodded.

"So you're the lady deputy I've heard about in all the local gossip these past months," said George. To Jane's surprise he held out his hand towards her. She walked over and squatted next to him as Ralph had done, and shook his hand.

"Jane Fleming," she said.

"George Robbins," he said. "I've sure wanted to see you for real, but I don't need to get to town much."

"Well, I'm for real, though most people in town would rather I wasn't," said Jane.

"Don't you let those small-minded idiots get you down," said George robustly, "If you're good at something and you wanna do it, you do it, no matter what anybody else says."

"Thank you Mr. Robbins," said Jane, touched, "You're only about the third person in this whole town in all this time who has been behind me like this."

"You call me George," he said warmly. Then he glanced with disdain at his situation. "It would have to be like this I finally meet you."

"Can you move at all George?" Jane asked.

"Nope. I tried going in and coming out. Can't budge either way."

Jane studied the situation seriously a moment.

"How about turning over? Can you turn on your back?"

George looked surprised at this, then attempted to turn to his left. Quite easily he turned around to where he was on his back, and a little ways further out the window.

A half a minute later Ralph and Edna came out of the house just as Jane was helping George to his feet. Ralph and Edna stopped in shock as George rubbed his stomach.

"Well, don't just stand there Edna! Go in and call the fire department back and tell them we don't need them," her husband commanded.

Edna jumped a little in surprise and then scurried back into the house. Ralph continued to stare at George and Jane.

"How did you get him out?" he asked Jane, "Did you pull him out?"

"Yes Ralph. This little woman pulled out this 250 pound man," said George sarcastically. Then he looked at Jane and smiled warmly. "She used her head Ralph. Figured I could twist my way out, and it worked." George offered his hand to Jane again. "Thank you Jane."

"You're welcome George," said Jane, shaking his hand.

Ralph went into complete shock at this exchange.

"Yep, you got a fine deputy here, Ralph," said George turning to him, "You should be glad to have her on your force." George walked past Ralph on his way to the back door and patted Ralph on the arm, bidding him farewell. Then he looked at Jane and said good-bye to her. She replied the same and George walked into the house.

Jane adjusted her hat. "Shall we go now Sheriff? I'll write up the report on this before going to see Mrs. Ballard," she said.

Jane's words jolted Ralph out of his daze.

"Yes. Of course Deputy," he said, still a little surprised.

He followed Jane back to the patrol cars and they each got in. Jane backed out first, only didn't wait for Ralph to back out so she would be following him. She turned the car and started back up Shady Lane, with Ralph following her.

By the time Jane finished writing up the report on the Robbins call, and transferred her notes from the O'Brien and friends' interviews to Jennie's file, it was close to four o'clock. This was the time Jane knew most the housewives were starting to prepare dinner, Mrs. Ballard no doubt being no exception. Jane was sure how she would take to having her supper preparations interrupted, but Jane was counting on these preparations to get the answers to the unusual questions she needed to ask Mrs. Ballard.

The smells coming through the house to the porch told Jane she was right about Mrs. Ballard preparing dinner. She rang the doorbell and waited. Several moments later Mrs. Ballard opened the door and stared at Jane through the screen door very annoyed.

"Mrs. Ballard. I would like to ask you a few questions regarding your son Steve," said Jane.

Mrs. Ballard scowled. "I can't answer any questions now. I'm right in the middle of making dinner."

"Yes Ma'am. But you can continue while I ask the questions. There aren't many."

Mrs. Ballard sighed. "Does this have to do with Jennie's disappearance?"

Jane wondered what else she thought it would be.

"Yes Ma'am."

Still perturbed at the interruption but her sense of priority altered, Mrs. Ballard pushed open the screen door for Jane.

"Come in."

Jane followed her through the house to the quaint country kitchen, accented in blue and brown and little geese. Mrs. Ballard went back to the salad she was preparing at the counter, while near her on the stove several pots boiled away and the oven was heard humming. From it came the smell of meat loaf.

"Okay. What do you want to ask?" said Mrs. Ballard, slicing away at a large radish.

"Mrs. Ballard, what time did Steve come in on the night of Jennie's disappearance?" asked Jane, with her pen and notepad in hand.

Mrs. Ballard looked up a split second, then back to her radish.

"Nine thirty," she said.

"And what time did he leave the house?"

"Seven thirty."

"So he was gone for two hours," said Jane, looking at Mrs. Ballard closely. She seemed more concerned with her salad than Jane's comment, which was what Jane was hoping for, and she only made an agreeing sound in her throat

"Did you ask him why he was home a half hour early, when his curfew was ten o'clock?" asked Jane.

"No. My husband and I didn't see him come in. We were watching television in the living room and Steve came in the back door."

"Is that usual?"

Mrs. Ballard now took a green onion and began chopping it.

"Is what usual?"

"Steve coming in the back door."

"No. He usually comes in the front door. But we heard him come in and my husband called out, and he said he was home, and we heard him run upstairs from the kitchen here."

Mrs. Ballard made a quick nod to the stairway on the other side of the kitchen which lead to the second floor. Jane noticed it, then turned back to Mrs. Ballard.

"Someone can go upstairs from here without being seen from the rest of the house?" asked Jane.

Mrs. Ballard scooped up the chopped green onion with her hand and dumped it in the salad.

"That's right."

Mrs. Ballard now began peeling some potatoes briskly. Jane let her get involved with a large one before asking her next question.

"Do you recall what Steve was wearing the night of Jennie's disappearance?"

"What he was wearing? Oh, that's easy enough to remember. Brown slacks, a white shirt, and the brand new beige pullover sweater he got from his Aunt Grace for his birthday. I remember because he looked so good in it, and he didn't wear a jacket because the sweater was heavy enough to keep him warm."

"He didn't wear a jacket?" asked Jane.

"No."

Jane flipped over a sheet in her notepad while watching Mrs. Ballard finish with the potato she was peeling. But she spoke before Mrs. Ballard could start on another.

"Could I see the sweater, Mrs. Ballard?" asked Jane.

Still distracted enough by her preparations for dinner yet in the midst of a slight pause, Mrs. Ballard looked briefly at Jane, then up the stairs.

"Well, I'll have to go get it from his room," she said.

Knowingly, Jane waited as Mrs. Ballard wiped her hands on a dish cloth and walked up the stairs. She was gone several minutes and Jane heard noises in all parts of the section she went in. Finally she came down with a puzzled expression on her face.

"Well that's funny, but I can't find it," she said, "It's not hanging up in his closet and it's not in the dirty clothes hamper."

"That's all right Mrs. Ballard," said Jane, preparing to leave, putting away her pen and notepad. "You can let me know when you find it."

"Oh yes. Of course," said Mrs. Ballard, preoccupied now with thinking about the missing sweater.

"Thank you for your cooperation," said Jane.

"You're welcome. And I'll ask Steve about the sweater. That's his brand new one from his Aunt Grace and it's expensive. I don't want anything to have happened to it."

Jane did not want this development, yet, and she looked at Mrs. Ballard firmly.

"I'll let you get back to your dinner preparations," Jane said emphatically.

Like a light switch turned off, Mrs. Ballard's preoccupation with the sweater disappeared and all her attention went back to her food.

"Oh yes. I'd better get the rest of those potatoes peeled and cooking. Bill and Steve will be coming home soon and they both like their supper served promptly at five."

"Good-bye Mrs. Ballard," said Jane, heading for the living room and the front door.

"Good-bye," said Mrs. Ballard, again so involved with her dinner preparations she didn't hear Jane leave through the front door.

CHAPTER SEVEN

If the softball league officials believed they were reflecting the sentiments of the people by wanting to cancel the evening's softball playoffs, they were wrong. You couldn't tell by the size of the crowd that anyone believed the games should be postponed because of Pops' murder. Bath the home and away bleachers of Huber Field were filling with softball fans from Pokagan, Marcellus and Grangeville. On the Grangeville side several fans painted a long sheet of paper with "Go Pit Bulls!" in flaming red and had it hanging from the top of the wire wall that ran the length of the top bleachers. Excitement filled the air, as did the smells of hot dogs, popcorn peanuts, cotton candy, caramel and candied apples and other snacks being sold from the portable concession stands and vans surrounding the diamond. The twilight was cool but not briskly so, so no heavy coats or sweaters were needed to watch the games.

In her sweatshirt, jeans and tennis shoes Jane looked like any other softball fan and not a Sheriff's deputy, so no one from Grangeville threw a second glance as she walked around the concession area with Butch. The crowd had the championship game on their minds and nothing else, not Jane, the female deputy nor Pops' death. True, these were mostly all young people and not ones to dwell on anyone's death, no matter how beloved to the town, nor on Jane's occupation when she wasn't wearing her uniform to remind them of it. Clark and several other Grangeville deputies on the evening shift were there to watch the crowd, but even they had more of their attention of the upcoming game than any crowd control that might be needed.

Clark actually smiled at and greeted Jane when she and Butch passed him in the concession area, and not because Clark was trying not to irritate Butch, but because Clark was excited and he saw someone he knew who was sharing his excitement. Jane smiled back and savored the first true, untainted exchange between her and Clark.

Butch was holding her hand as they walked down one of the aisles the stands and vans formed around the field. He wore his Pit Bulls uniform and cap, and tonight Jane thought he never looked as handsome or appealing as he did now in that outfit. She was caught up in the excitement too and after the depressing events that had happened in town and the work she was assigned of finding Jennie O'Brien, she was even more susceptible to the free-wheeling atmosphere surrounding her. But it wasn't this which made Butch look so good to her tonight. She just realized tonight just how much she was in love with the man.

As they walked people would pause and call out greetings to Butch, not only people from Grangeville but Pokagan and Marcellus, too. Butch would nod and smile and reply back in a clever and witty way. Jane felt a strong spurt of feminine pleasure at being Butch's girl, at being seen by his side, after each greeting. Whether Butch's team won or lost, tonight for Jane was going to be remembered as a wonderful night.

"You haven't had dinner yet, have you Janie?" said Butch as they came upon a hot dog stand. Jane shook her head no and Butch lead her by the hand up to the edge of it.

"Two dogs, with everything on them," he said to the large man behind the counter. The man quickly handed them the hot dogs and wished Butch good luck tonight as Butch paid him. As they bit into the dogs they walked across to a soft drink stand and Butch ordered two Pepsis.

"Wouldn't you like a beer instead, Butch?" asked Jane, glancing at the beer stand near the soft drink one.

Butch shook his head.

"Sex before a game is fine. But beer? No," he said.

They finished the dogs and drinks and then Butch bought them each a caramel apple. Jane turned hers over and over a few times with a confused look on her face.

"I never know where to start these things," said Jane, "When are they gang to start putting a 'Bite here' on them?"

Butch chuckled, caramel on his mouth from where he had bit into his apple. Jane finally bit but brushed her nose against some of the caramel and got some of the sticky stuff on it.

"Oh geez," she said, attempting to wipe it off but only smearing it more. Butch chuckled again and Waned down to wipe the caramel off her nose with his tongue and lips. The action tickled Jane and she giggled. Butch heard the giggle and when finished with the caramel moved his lips to hers and kissed her, the apple's juice and the caramel and their saliva all mixing together and all tasting very good to them.

"Good evening," a voice said suddenly, and Jane and Butch interrupted their kiss to see to whom it belonged. Tim Usher stood in front of them, and he had a pleasant but slightly odd smile on his face.

"Hello Tim," said Jane, smiling warmly in return.

"How ya doin', Usher old man," said Butch, and offered his hand.

"Good," said Tim, but not exactly firm in his declaration as he shook Butch's hand.

"Are you here covering the games for the paper?" asked Jane, before taking another small bite of her caramel apple.

"Yes," replied Tim.

"Care to sit with us?" asked Butch.

"thanks, but I'll be sitting in the press box by the Visitors' dugout," Tim said.

"Well, join us at the victory celebration afterwards at Uncle Nunizo's."

Tim studied Butch with just the slightest bit of animosity that nether Jane or Butch, in the happy and loving mood each was in because of the other, noticed.

"You're really sure you're gonna win?" said Tim, with that animosity now in his tone.

"It's in the bag, my friend," said Butch confidently.

Tim's animosity dropped from him slowly as he stood there looking at Butch. Then a genuinely warm smile crossed his face.

"Well, I want to wish you good luck with the game, anyway,' said Tim.

"Thanks," said Butch.

"Bye Jane," said Tim, turning his glance to her.

"Bye," said Jane, and Tim left, disappearing into the crowd.

"Nice guy," said Butch, taking a bite of his apple now.

"He's a good friend," said Jane.

The lights around Huber Field sprang on, signaling the first game was to start. Immediately the crowd around the concession area left and began to fill in the bleachers of the appropriate team. The Grangeville fans sat on the bleachers facing north, and the Pokagan and Marcellus fans sat in the ones facing west.

Huber Field was about a half mile from the center of Grangeville, on the other side of town from Pebble Creek. The announcer's stand was perpendicular to the Grangeville bleachers, and the dugouts for the teams were in front of each of the stands, which were filling quickly. Butch bought Jane and himself a box of popcorn and another Pepsi, and they joined the fans in the Grangeville bleachers. Since Butch and his team would not be playing till the outcome of the first game was known, they sat within their fans, noticeable by their white uniforms patterned after the home ones of the Detroit Tigers. Jane sat between Butch and Sy, who did not play for Butch's team, but for his employer's, the Evans Lumberyard Yankees, who came in second again in the division this year behind Butch's Pit Bulls. After losing out like this last year and again this, Sy declared he was going to join Butch's team next year and win, whether Mr. Evans liked it or not.

Andy French sat nearby, as did Wilbur (Call me Wil) Lawson, both also of Butch's team. The rest of the Pit Bulls sat scattered around the bleachers with their family and friends.

"So who do you want to see win, Butch?" asked Sy, leaning around Jane slightly to get a clearer view of Butch.

"Don't matter to me. The Pit Bulls can take either team," said Butch, munching on his popcorn nonchalantly and sitting with his elbows on his knees.

Pete Schmidt, in his Pit Bulls uniform, walked to the middle of the softball field just behind second base where a microphone was being set up by a Grangeville High student, followed by another student carrying a trumpet. Pete was to sing the national anthem, and as he situated himself in front of the microphone and the trumpet player raised his horn next to Pete's shoulder, the public address system crackled on and Lloyd Bunker, the long time announcer of all of Grangeville's softball games, spoke.

"Will you all please rise and join in our national anthem," he said.

Everyone in both bleachers stood almost in unison and all the players removed their caps. Pete glanced at the trumpet player and together they began to perform the anthem.

Jane sang along softly, mainly because she was not much of a singer, but mostly to hear Butch. Butch was not a bad singer, when he put his mind to it, and tonight he was putting forth some effort to sing well, Jane's guess as to his reason was to help his friend Pete along, if only in spirit. Pete had a strong tenor voice with an appealing scratchiness underneath it, and when he finished with the anthem the crowd gave him and the trumpet player a thundering ovation. Pete made a little nod of his head and waved his cap enthusiastically.

As Pete and the trumpet player and the student with the microphone walked off the field, the umpires trotted out on the field and took their positions. The crowd began to chatter again and Lloyd sounded over the P.A. again.

"Ladies and Gentlemen, welcome to the Cass County Amateur Softball League Championship Playoff!" he said, building with each word to an enthusiastic gusto. The crowd applauded him. "The first game tonight will be between the Van Lacken Tool & Die Indians from Pokagan and the Wheeler's Bar & Grill Marauders from Marcellus. Winner will then play the defending champions, the Przybylski Garage and Filling Station Pit Bulls from Grangeville."

The Grangeville fans went crazy with noise at the mention of their team. The fans on the top bleachers, the one who had put up the sign, began chanting, "Butch, Butch, Butch," in an exaggerated deep tone. They kept it up and were so loud Butch was finally urged by Sy to acknowledge them. Butch stood, turned to the top back row of bleachers and doffed his cap towards it. The fans, all young men, cheered heartily for him. When Butch sat back down next to her, Jane was smiling broadly and she grabbed his arm and squeezed it. Butch looked surprised at Jane's action, but then looked quite pleased and kissed her.

Lloyd announced each team member, and they trotted out to stand along either the first or third base line. When Lloyd finished, the lines broke and the Indians came up to bat.

Each team was here to play, as Butch quipped at about the third inning, as the hits and outs and runs were chalked up quickly and fairly evenly between the two teams. But in the end the Van Lacken Tool & Die Indians emerged victorious by two runs.

The Grangeville fans cheered wildly when Butch and his teammates began to file off the bleachers to begin their warm-ups for the championship game. Jane gave Butch a kiss for luck before he left her side.

The other two teams left the field, and a group of a dozen or so flashily costumed young women took their place. A woman slightly older stood off to the side and applauded the girls vigorously, and shouted out something to them.

"Lades and Gentlemen, before the start of the next game, for your entertainment, the Grangeville High Creative Dance Class will perform an interpretation of the hit song, 'Brandy' by the Looking Glass group," came Lloyd's voice over the P.A.

A few seconds after he finished, the scratching noise of the beginning of a record was heard over the air and the girls scurried into two lines, one facing ft Grangeville bleachers and the other the Pokagan-Marcellus ones. They all stood in the same position, their left leg bent and their knee held in the air, and their batons across their chests. The girls' excitement and enthusiasm could be seen on their faces by everyone in the bleachers, excitement and enthusiasm shared by their teacher off to the side.

The music and words of the song began, and the girls went into their routine. For all their effort and sincerity, they were pretty poor creative dancers. Or at least what they were creating couldn't have been what they had planned. Two or three dropped their batons in the midst of the routine, and one fell. Jane turned to look at Sy next to her and her expression was both amused and incredulous. Sy was biting his lower lip so hard it was white, but when he and Jane looked at each other neither could control themselves and they burst out laughing, fighting hard to keep it low, though. The reactions of the other fans on both bleachers were not much different, except some were not as polite nor amused and began to catcall nasty remarks down to the girls. Butch's fan club at the top began to make disgusting animal-like noises at the girls, in between chants for the game. Some of the girls on the field heard or saw some of the reactions of their audience, and their looks began to express a good deal of hurt. Their teacher however showed nothing but pleasure and thrill at the girls' performance, and encouraged them on with her body language.

Suddenly from the dugout ran the Przybylski Pit Bulls, complete with bats, balls and gloves, lead by Butch, and with no notice of the dancing girls, began to throw, bat, and pitch to each other on the field. Pete trotted out to left field and Butch began shagging a few balls to him. The crowd mostly cheered at their appearance, but the dancing teacher went into a fit. She ran around the diamond like a shot right up to Butch.

From her seat high in the bleachers Jane could see the teacher grab Butch's arm and pull him strongly to face her. Her words could not be heard over the music and the noise of the crowd but from the expression on her face and the shade of red it suddenly got it was obvious she was reading Hutch the riot act. She pointed to the girls still performing on the field and waving her arms wildly. Butch could be seen only staring at her expressionless, her words not appearing to register with him. Finally he looked disgusted at the barrage the teacher was giving him, and he signaled to his team to gather in off the field. They did so and lined up in front of the dugout waiting for the girls to finish. Jane looked over at

Butch standing off by himself. His thought of: "Get these damn broads off the field so we can play some ball" was clearly on his face as he leaned on his bat and crossed one leg over the other, watching the girls. And Jane knew at that moment she never loved Butch more.

Mercifully the song soon ended, and the girls marched off the field to only a scattering of polite applause. Butch's fan club began some loud hoots, a mixture of displeasure at the girls and enthusiasm that the game would now start. The umpires took their places again and the Van Lacken Indians lined back up at the first base line. Lloyd came over the P.A. system again.

"Ladies and Gentlemen, I world like to introduce now the reigning Softball League Champions. The Przybylski Pit Bulls."

The Grangeville bleachers went wild and everyone stood, including Jane, applauding wildly.

"At first base, Peter Schmidt."

Pete trotted out and the fans applauded.

"Second base, Andy French"

Again, Andy came out and received applause.

"Shortstop, Wil Lawson."

Each player was called and their position, and the crowd showed their approval. Then it was time to announce the starting pitcher for the Pit Bulls.

"Pitcher, and captain and sponsor of the Pit Bulls, Butch Przybylski."

Butch came out and the Grangeville fans went wild. They stood, applauded, stomped their feet, someone even tossed a handful of confetti in the air. Jane watched him take his place next to the catcher, take off his cap and wave it; all the while she applauded along with the crowd. A big, loving smile crossed her face.

The home plate umpire called out the play ball, and the Pit Bulls being the home team, the first batter who stepped up to the plate was an Indian. Butch stood on the pitcher's mound and caught the ball his catcher, Lonnie Sargeant, threw out to him. The batter, catcher and umpire took their stance while Butch threw the ball repeatedly into this glove. His jaw was moving up and down vigorously and from the stands Jane saw him blow a large bubble from his gum. When it popped and he sucked the gum back into his mouth he went into his stance, read Lonnie's signals and fired in a pitch. It was a fastball and it whizzed past the Indian batter and the umpire yelled out "Strike!"

The Grangeville fans roared their approval. Butch proved to Jane he was right not to worry about having sex with her this afternoon. Butch was devastating on the mound tonight. He scattered only three hits in the first six innings and drove in a run and hit a homer himself in the second and third. By the seventh inning the scoreboard on the field read: Grangeville: five, Visitors: zero.

By the middle of the Indians' half of the seventh inning Butch seemed to be practically untouchable. Then the Indians' third baseman came out. He was a big, heavyset young man, who would have looked more in place on the football field than on the softball diamond. A trace of anger was still in his eyes at Butch for striking him out with three straight pitches his last at-bat. The Indian took his stance after a few swings and looked at Butch with narrowed eyes.

The batter's look did not register with Butch, who circled the mound a few times before standing and reading Lonnie's signals. Butch wound up, looked at home plate, and let a high hard fastball fly.

The Indians' batter was not going to let Butch get another one by him and he swung madly and wildly at the ball. It contacted the bat and went out with just about the same amount of speed as it came in, and headed straight back to Butch. Before he could move or do anything, the ball hit him right in the groin.

Jane leaped to her feet but her view of Butch disappeared as those in front of her leaped up too and stood on the benches. Sy, being over six feet tall, still kept a clear view of the field when he stood.

"Oh my God!" said Sy, with agony in his voice.

"Oh Sy, is he all right!" cried Jane. She jumped on her bench too and leaned on Sy to stand tiptoe. On the field Butch was on his knees, his back to first base, and his hands clutching at the spot between his legs. Pete from first base reached him first and bent over him.

"Sy, do you think I should go down there?" asked Jane worriedly. Butch disappeared from view when the rest of his team came in from their positions and surrounded him.

"Wait a minute Jane, maybe he's not too badly hurt," said Sy.

Jane looked at him wide-eyed.

"Sy, didn't you see where he got hit?" said Jane.

"Jane, I saw it and I felt it," said Sy knowingly.

The home plate umpire soon joined the Pit Bulls as they surrounded their fallen leader. There was a look of concern on his face but also just the tiniest bit of black humor.

"Is he gonna be all right, fellas?" he asked.

To the umpire's utter surprise, Butch immediately rose to his feet and straightened easily. He looked at the umpire right in the eyes.

"Barely fazed me, Ump," he said.

The umpire looked completely stunned at Butch, then shrugged and started back for home plate.

Both Jane and the crowd let out an audible sigh of relief when the Pit Bulls left the mound and Butch was seen standing straight and tall with no sign of pain in his body or on his face. When the game resumed, Butch eyed the batter, who had attempted to take away his manhood and who had made it safety to first base, with a deadly gleam in his eye as the next batter came up. Butch handled that one easily, but kept throwing to Pete at first, trying to pick the runner off. Finally the Indian, getting cocky from the way Butch kept missing throwing him out, which was exactly why Butch was throwing that way, went too far off first base and with lightening speed Butch threw to first and nabbed him. The Grangeville crowd roared its approval and Butch watched with a satisfied smirk as the Indian walked back to the dugout.

The Pit Bulls and Butch were unstoppable for the rest of the game, and when the final pop fly was caught by Wil Lawson, the score read nine to zero and the Pit Bulls retained their championship. The Grangeville fans went crazy and some began pouring onto the field. His teammates all came running up to Butch again, this time to shake his hand and each other's. Butch was grinning broadly as he accepted their handshakes and congratulations and the pats on the back he received from the fans. But there was one particular grab of his arm that brought his attention to that person. He saw her and immediately dropped his glove, and took Jane into his arms and lifted her off her feet so she was eye to eye with him, and kissed her hard.

It was about half an hour before the fans were persuaded by Lloyd to leave the field and resume their seats so the trophy presentation could be held. The president of the softball league, a Mr. Almaguer who was a bank loan officer from Marcellus, stood with Butch, the rest of the Pit Bulls and a few fans who didn't return to their seats, on the pitcher's mound. The student with the microphone had returned and was holding the mike in front of Mr. Almaguer. Mr. Almaguer held the tall championship trophy.

"I would like to offer my congratulations to the Przybylski Pit Bulls on winning and so retaining the Cass County Amateur Softball League Championship. And present to their captain, this trophy."

He handed Butch the trophy and Butch accepted it, and shook Mr. Almaguer's offered hand, all while the Grangeville fans cheered. The student turned and held the mike in front of Butch earnestly, handling the situation very seriously. Butch eyed the trophy and looked a little humble.

"On behalf of my teammates and myself, I thank you for this trophy. And a special thanks to all our Grangeville fans. Grangeville fans are the greatest fans in the world!" Butch looked up to them with these words, which he spoke with great enthusiasm. The crowd cheered again and Butch held the trophy high over his head with one hand. While with the other he reached around and put it around Jane, who stood next to him. When he had her in his grip he looked down to her and kissed her yet again. Then after the full but brief kiss Butch looked up to the fans again and spoke into the microphone.

"Last ones to Uncle Nunzio's drinks warm beer!" he bellowed lustfully.

***

Some fans were already at Uncle Nunzio's and far into the partying when Butch, Jane, Pete and the rest of the Pit Bulls arrived from Huber Field to celebrate. The crowd cheered Butch and the Pit Bulls as they walked through the restaurant, Butch holding the trophy high with one hand. Uncle Nunzio's owner, who was a man named Ray McKinney, had a table all set for the Pit Bulls and their guests, and they sat around it when they reached it. Ray and one of his waitresses brought several pitchers of beer to the table and began to fill the large mugs set out before the Pit Bulls.

After the first pitchers had been drained and the pizzas ordered and eaten and all the fans who wanted to came up and congratulated the Pit Bulls, calm settled in on the group and they lingered over their refilled beers. They rehashed the whole game and pointed out what they could have done better and what they still had to work on as a team.

"Well, it was a great game, but Butch, I don't know how you played after getting that ball in your balls," said Pete, who usually wouldn't have been that colorful with his words except he was feeling good after all that beer.

Butch, who was sitting back in his chair, one arm around the back of Jane's next to it and the other bringing a small cigar to his mouth to smoke, grinned mockingly smug.

"They don't call me Ironman Przybylski for nothin'," said Butch, "Don't you know I have the pain threshold of ten men?"

Those sitting around the table all laughed, including Jane, but afterwards she leaned in to Butch. He leaned in to her at seeing the expression on her face.

"But are you all right Butch?" she whispered, and gently slipped her hand on his thigh, not in a sexual move but a nursing, caressing one.

"I'll show you later on just how all right I am," said Butch slyly. But then his tone became sincere when he saw a small amount of concern in

Jane's eyes. "He didn't actually hit me *there*, it was more in the left thigh. It only looked like he got me in the family jewels.

Complete relief now came into Jane's eyes, and she and Butch began to kiss tenderly, repeatedly.

"Hey, can we get in on this celebration or it is restricted only to you two?" said Pete boisterously. Butch and Jane looked away from each other to Pete but remained with their heads close together.

"You can't possibly be as good a kisser as Jane, Pete," said Butch, "We've worked together a long time and practically everyday but I've never got the impression I'd wanna kiss you."

Pete went into a buzzed laughing jag which spread to the others in the group except Butch and Jane, who kissed again instead.

"Hey, I almost thought I found the Pebble Creek Pit up there the other day, when I was there fishing," said Wil, after draining his beer mug and while refilling it from pitcher.

"The Pebble Creek Pit?" said Jane, the mention of Pebble Creek arousing a Sheriff's business thought in her.

Butch made a sound of disgust and disbelief as he leaned back and smoked his cigar. Jane looked at him and then back at Wil.

"What's that?" she asked.

"You mean no one's ever told you yet about the Pebble Creek Pit Legend?" said Wil, "Not even Butch?"

"I've got better things to talk to Jane about then some asinine legend," he said.

Jane, her attention now thoroughly captured by the topic, waved her hand briskly at Butch, then turned back to Wil.

"What about this pit?" she asked.

"Well, nobody knows if it really exits, nobody's ever found it," said Wil, "But it's suppose to be somewhere in the Pebble Creek area and its bottomless and…" Wil paused for dramatic effect, and got it from his listeners, "It harbors this incredibly huge, incredibly ugly, incredibly strong, incredibly dangerous, incredibly smelly, creature that comes out of the pit late on certain nights and roams the area, tearing apart whatever living creature it gets its powerful claws on, then disappears back into the pit just before sunrise."

Everyone around the table reacted in shivering delicious horror to the story, despite the fact that it was familiar to them since childhood. Everyone, except Butch and Jane. Jane stared as she absorbed the legend for the first time, while Butch rolled his eyes in exasperation and blew out another long draw of the cigar smoke up and over to the side.

"No one's ever seen the creature, but people have found strange shapes in the dirt and sand up there around Pebble Creek that they attribute to it," continued Wil with great spooking effect.

"Yeah, instead of two people lying on the ground making out," said Butch.

"Shhhhh" said Jane quickly to Butch. Butch only shrugged at her and took a swallow of beer.

"But what about the pit?" asked Jane firmly.

Wil shrugged, his tone turning realistic again.

"The story is that about thirty years ago the pit was found, and filled in." Wil's tone then returned to its former spooky style. "But no one knew who found it or who filled it in, so maybe it was never found and maybe it was never filled in," he added.

"And no maybes about it, it never existed," said Butch with conviction.

Ray McKinney came up just then, and informed the Pit Bulls and their guests that it was two A.M., and time for him to close up. After one last salute with the last of their beer, the partygoers broke up their gathering and left Ray to lock up.

Butch drove with his left hand on the wheel and his other arm stretched out behind the seat beside him. Jane sat right next to him and her head rested lazily and cozily on his shoulder, but her mind was churning. Butch drove home slowly because the day's activities had finally caught up with him and he was tired, but mainly because the night was autumn crisp, clear and cool, and a large October Harvest moon hung low in the sky they were headed at. The country road they drove on was deserted, and soft music emitted from the glowing car radio.

Jane sighed softly.

"Butch," she then said quietly.

"Yes," he replied, also quietly.

"Are you really sure there isn't a pit out somewhere in Pebble Creek?" she asked.

"Yes," said Butch softly but firmly, "It's just some dumb, half-baked story somebody made up years ago to scare kids away from going up there to make out. Didn't even work at that."

"It is?"

"Jane, I've lived here in Grangeville all my life and I've been over practically every foot of Pebble Creek. There's no monstrous hole in the ground out there. And definitely no monster. All the monsters live right in town. And we just lost the biggest one a couple of days ago."

Jane didn't need for Butch to explain who that was he was talking about. But it fit in with the thoughts that had been swirling around in her head a moment before. The idea that Jennie O'Brien had fallen in that supposed hole in Pebble Creek during her flight from Steve crossed her mind when Wil Lawson mentioned the hole this evening. And she had seriously thought for a moment it was a real possibility that was what happened to Jennie, instead of her original theory. But with Butch's repeated firm conviction against there being any hole it made her reject the new theory completely. And it didn't explain the clue that had led her to her original theory in the first place.

With this now settled, her mind relaxed and she absorbed the magic and beauty of the night before her and Butch. The finely tuned engine produced a lulling hum as the car chased down the finely graveled road. She snuggled closer to Butch and she felt him put his arm closer around her shoulder.

The Mustang pulled up to Butch's house and parked. Butch cut the motor, but left the ignition turned on so that the radio stayed on. They were now sitting with the moon before them hanging in the sky. Jane started to get out but Butch grabbed her and pulled her back.

"Wait a minute. Let's sit here for a while," he said.

Jane offered no argument but happily sat back against him.

"I'm so proud of you, Butch," Jane said.

"For winning the softball championship tonight?" he asked.

"That too. But proud…of you, yourself, and of everything you do. All the time. I think you're a special guy and I'm so lucky you're my fella."

Jane didn't see it but Butch blushed a little. She took his arms that were around her and pulled them tighter. Her head rested back further on his chest.

"I don't know if I ever told you this Butch, but if it weren't for you, I wouldn't have gotten through those first weeks in the Sheriff's Department. I know I would have given up and quit if you hadn't been there to pull me through. And even now, when I have a bad time."

Her words made Butch absolutely speechless for a few moments till he broke through it with humor.

"You make me sound like St. Butch," he said.

Jane laughed softly. They sat silently a few minutes as the moon rose higher in the sky.

"I'm awfully proud of you, Janie. I can't take all the credit, you've hung in there too and showed all those SOBs you've got what it takes to be a cop." Butch lowered his head and spoke into Jane's hair. "I think you're very special too. And you make me happier than any man has a right to be." He paused a few seconds and rubbed his cheek against her hair. "Janie, I've been thinking. We should make what we got legal. Before the town gets too complacent about us. We should do something to shake them up again. Jane, how about we get…"

Butch stopped. Something felt unusual about Jane. Carefully Butch turned her and saw she had fallen asleep. With a grin he turned off the car and to not disturb Jane slowly got out. He opened the front door then came back to the car and picked Jane up in his arms. She didn't move but continued sleeping, all the way through Butch carrying her into the house and to the bedroom.

CHAPTER EIGHT

Jane woke very early the next morning to Butch's face looming completely over hers. It was barely light out but there was enough of it in the room for her to see Butch's sly, smirking expression. As Jane stirred she felt herself wearing Butch's pajama top and automatically knew Butch was wearing the bottom. She felt so warm and secure with her head deep in the pillows and her body under the sheet, blankets and quilt and next to Butch's big-framed body, a contented drowsy smile crossed her face.

"Good morning sleepyhead," said Butch quietly.

"What time is it?" whispered Jane.

"Only five-thirty."

"Oh good," said Jane, as she brought her arms up from under the covers and placed them around Butch's neck. She drew him to her and they kissed, gently at first, then intensifying. Butch moved completely over her and Jane felt him reach down and pull open his pajama bottom at the crotch, allowing him to function more freely. And function Butch did. Jane was so awed at his actions it made her unable to move as strongly as she regularly did and she laid mostly complacent. But her inner responses were far from complacent and were actually twice as intense as they usually were. She cried out Butch's name several times, and was much more verbal than usual. When they finally finished and Butch moved slightly to the side from Jane but still right above her, Jane glanced at the clock on the right stand next to the bed. The clock said it was 6:37 A.M.

"You convinced now I wasn't hurt last night by that line drive to the dick?" Butch asked, turning his head from the pillow and looking at her with one eye as he still panted deeply.

"Oh, yes, Butch," said Jane, finding it hard to put words together.

" I wanted to show you last night, but you fell asleep in the car," he said, now closer to a more normal pace of breathing. He rose up on his elbows and looked down at Jane, and smiled a warm, genuine smile.

"Well, I don't remember putting this on," said Jane, touching the lapel of the pajama top

"I put it on you. And I must admit it was a lot of fun. Almost as much as taking the clothes off."

Butch smiled again. And Jane felt the surge of feminine pleasure again at just being with him, and now in this special place, his bed. She took his head in her hands and Butch shut his eyes, and she Puttered him, and then he kissed her closed eyes in return. Then Jane ran her fingers through the plentiful hair on his chest, lingering delicately a little at each place with her fingertips. This made Butch intake his breath sharply several times, but he didn't move and he let her continue doing it.

"Like this?" asked Jane.

"Uh huh," said Butch, "And there's something else I'd like even more."

"What's that?"

"A backrub. I'm kind of achy from playing last right."

"Then lie down," said Jane. Butch proceeded to do so then Jane climbed on him, straddling his hips.

"Where does it bother you the most?" asked Jane, as she began to massage its neck.

"My shoulder blades."

Jane drew her fingers downward to Butch's powerful shoulder blades and firmly began to massage them. Butch, his head resting on its side and his hands under his cheek, let out a low, pleasurable groan.

"Must be from alt the fast balls you threw yesterday," commented Jane.

She finished a few minutes later, after massaging all of Butch's back. Then she climbed off Butch's waist and made moves to climb out of bed.

"I'll go put on the coffee and why don't you go start your shower," said Jane. But Butch grabbed her hand before she made it even close to getting out of bed and stopped her.

"I've got a better idea. Why don't I go put on the coffee and you wait here in bed for me," he said.

"What about your shower, and mine?" asked Jane.

"We'll make up the time by taking them together," said Butch. He forced Jane back under the covers and got up himself. As he stretched the elastic around the waist of his pajama bottom, he walked around the bed and out the bedroom door, Jane watched him from her position of lying back on the bed. She watched intently every movement every inch of his lanky, yet strong, firm body made till he left the room, and Jane marveled again at what an incredibly special man Butch was, and how fortunate she was he chose her to be with.

But as she laid there and heard Butch moving around the kitchen and talking to Jesse and letting him outside and the smell of freshly brewing coffee began to permeate the room; the same dark quirk of fear she felt at the LaPierre suddenly nipped at Jane of what she would do if Butch ever called it quits with her. Her breath caught in her throat and her heart actually pounded a little harder in her chest. It lasted only a few moments, though, as Butch seemed to be doing something else in the kitchen besides making the coffee and Jane's curiosity blanketed over her fear. She listened carefully trying to figure out from the sounds what he was doing, but found out ten minutes later when Butch came back to the bedroom carrying a serving tray with two cups of coffee and hot waffles drowning in batter and maple syrup. As Jane sat up in surprise Butch set the tray over her lap.

"I thought you'd like some nourishment too, along with the coffee," said Butch.

"Oh Butch, this is lovely. But what about you?" asked Jane, picking up the napkin from under the silverware and laying it on her lap.

"I thought, maybe, you'd share your waffles with me," he said in a mock begging tone.

Jane looked up at Butch from lowered brows.

"C'mon in here, Big Guy," she said huskily.

Butch walked around the bed and climbed back in on his side. Jane cut a square of the waffle with her fork and swirled it around in the syrup. Then she offered it to Butch and he took it with his teeth. As he chewed

Jane took a bite herself. They looked at each other as they chewed and after swallowing, Butch leaned forward and kissed Jane, both their lips sticky and wet with the sweet syrup.

Butch shaved after showering with Jane, though it wasn't easy with Jane insisting she dry him oft while he lathered up his face and took a razor to it When her hand slipped into certain places it made him jump in start.

"Watch it Janie! You're gonna make me slit my throat!" he said.

"Oh I'm sorry. Here, I'm done now." And she made final rubbing motions on Butch in the place where he lined up with the waist-high sink.

Butch's eyes squinted together as she finished.

"You may be done now, but you've started something else," he said.

Grabbing her, he kissed her and got shaving cream all around her mouth. Dropping together onto the bathroom floor they completed the situation Jane started with her towel and then, Butch finished his shaving.

It was close to seven-thirty when Butch dropped Jane off at her apartment in town before driving to work himself. Jane went upstairs and chard into her Sheriff's uniform, then drove herself to the Sheriff's office. She was all business now and the effects of her morning with Butch properly aside in her mind. Of course she could do nothing about the look in her eyes and when she said good morning to Ralph, he saw it again and stiffened visibly.

"The Przybylski Pit Bulls retained their softball championship, did you hear, Sheriff?" said Jane, taking off her jacket and going to her desk.

"No, err...yes, I heard," said Ralph, pausing in his placement of wanted posters on the bulletin board.

"I'll pass along your congratulations to Butch," said Jane, sitting down.

This was one of the rare times she needled at Ralph just a little with his reaction to her relationship with Butch. The residual from the lovemaking with Butch this morning was just a little too powerful and crept out from the place in her mind she usually carefully kept it, and made her nudge a little at Ralph about his reaction, albeit very subtly. She knew just the mentioning of Butch would bother Ralph more, and the insinuation that she would be seeing Butch again sometime was another little dig that would add to it. And they both did. Ralph shuffled on his feet and grunted and cleared his throat several times. His face went slightly red, and Jane wondered as she studied Ralph's reaction just what he would do if she ever came out and told point blank she and Butch Przybylski were lovers. He'd probably have a heart attack.

"You do that, Deputy," Ralph finally got out. He almost thumb-tacked his finger onto the board as he spoke.

"I plan on interviewing Charlie O'Brien today, Sheriff, regarding his sister's disappearance. And I'd like to talk to Steve Ballard again." Jane saw what he almost did and dropped the understated teasing.

"Fine, Deputy," said Ralph.

"Sheriff," said Jane, standing suddenly, and in a tone and look that was totally serious, "Has there been any progress in the investigation of Pops Griffiths' murder?"

But the subject of the question and the answer completely changed Ralph's demeanor back to a serious law enforcement officer. He lost all embarrassment about Jane and looked at her fully, now with slight annoyance in his eyes and tone of voice, coming from the answer he had to give her.

"No, Deputy," he said sternly, "There's been no breakthrough on the Griffiths' murder investigation."

"It's been almost a week now," said Jane.

"I know that Deputy," Ralph slightly snapped, "I've got the man's only living relative coming here tomorrow and I don't have a damn thing to tell her about his murder, or the whole town who thought of him as a relative." Ralph gave a grunting sigh. "We've just hit a blank wall. Nobody's found a single lead we can follow up on."

Jane studied Ralph a few seconds.

"I hope I'll have one soon, Sheriff."

Ralph shot a sharp look at her.

'What do you mean? You aren't still thinking there's a connection between Pops' murder and the O'Brien girl's disappearance?"

"Yes, Sheriff," said Jane.

She expected Ralph to bellow on, but to her surprise he gestured away as he turned from her.

"Well, if you think so..." Ralph walked into his office and shut the door. Jane gave a small relieved sigh. Ralph wasn't convinced, yet at least he wasn't denying the possibility anymore. That was a small victory, but a victory nevertheless. Jane was certain very soon now she would be able to state her theory to Ralph regarding the connection, and why she brought up the subject of Pops' murder investigation, and this change of heart in him would help in convincing him her theory was true. She knew it was. And perhaps from Charlie O'Brien she would get that one piece of information she needed to finally stitch what she had together into a coherent picture.

On her way to the junior high to interview Charlie, she heard a call from Galen regarding an earlier call he responded to about some vandalism on a house on Southview Street. Jane had heard the call on her radio and his voice had been calm and controlled when he took it, but now it was raised a few octaves and he sounded on the verge of panic. Jane knew it didn't take much to throw Galen, but just in case it was serious, she radioed to him she was on her way to assist him.

Southview Street was where the better homes and more well-to-do families of Grangeville lived, and Jane drove past the big homes and finely kept, landscaped lawns till she came to the address Galen was called to. And she saw what the problem was, or at least why the Sheriff had been called. Over every bush, tree, shrub and flower bed someone had draped toilet paper. And whoever did it had done a thorough job. It looked like it had snowed on the lawn.

Galen's patrol car was parked in the driveway and Jane drove in behind it. As she got out of the car Galen got out of his. Jane surveyed the scene and grinned a little.

"Somebody jumped the gun on Devil's Night, I see," she said as Galen came trotting up to her quickly, "They must have really had it in for the people living here."

"This isn't funny, Jane!" said Galen in a harsh whisper, "The people here are furious!"

"I can imagine they are," said Jane. She looked at Galen fully now and saw he was completely shaken. "So did you take their report? And why did you call for back-up?"

Before Galen could answer, the front door to the house opened, and an impeccably groomed man, in his early forties and quite nice-looking, in a three piece suit, came storming out of the house and down the stone path to them in the driveway.

"Good! I'm glad you called for help," said the man. When he saw Jane he scowled a little. "But what kind of help is *she* going to be?" he snapped.

Immediately Jane was on the alert.

"I'm Deputy Jane Fleming, sir," she said, "And what's your name?"

"John Bylen," said the man.

"Now what's exactly the problem here, Mr. Bylen?" asked Jane.

Bylen's eyes practically popped out of his head.

"My lawn has been desecrated!" he bellowed.

"I can see that sir," said Jane, continuing to remain calm, "But why has Deputy Keyes called for back-up?"

Both Jane and Bylen turned to look at Galen. Under the scrutiny of them both he immediately began to tremble.

"Mr. Bylen, Mr. Bylen...wants...wants...Galen began, but Bylen broke in impatiently and finished the sentence for him.

"I want him to clean this yard up!" he said. And Galen nodded rapidly in agreement.

Jane looked startled for a second, then regained her poise.

"I'm sorry Mr. Bylen, that isn't something under our jurisdiction."

"You're public servants aren't you!" yelled Bylen, getting red in the face now, as Galen cowed. "You people are supposed to help the public! My wife is in hysterics, I had to stay hone from work this morning to handle this! I pay your salaries with my taxes!" Bylen added the latter sentence with bath great finesse and arrogance. When he saw none of this was making an impression on Jane, he took one last try. "This deputy said you would!"

Jane finally reacted to this.

"Oh, he did, did he?" she asked earnestly, "Well, then, I guess we'll have to do it."

Bylen looked quickly pleased while Galen's head jerked around to Jane and he looked startled at her. From the expression on his face he obviously had thought there was no way Jane, or anyone who had answered his back-up call, would actually help him clean up all the toilet paper. But Jane walked over to a nearby shrub and began to clear the flimsy sheets off the stiff branches. Bylen sighed quite satisfactorily and walked back into the house. Galen watched him go in, then went up to Jane.

"Thank, you, Jane," he said, "I owe you one."

"Just watch what you offer to do for the public next time," said Jane shortly, "That's how you can repay me." She wadded up the long trail of toilet paper that she pulled from the bottom of the shrub. "Now go up to the house and get us some trash bags to put this in."

"Right. Then I'll get started on the tree," said Galen earnestly, nodding to the medium-sized one on the lawn, where toilet paper strips fluttered in the slight breeze that was blowing. He ran up to the house and after speaking to Mrs. Bylen, who was now obviously over her hysterics about the T.P. job with the word from her husband the Sheriff's deputies would clean it up, returned to Jane with several large trash bags. Jane stuffed her bundle in one and started on another shrub.

Galen began clearing off the maple tree in the yard. It was slow, tedious work, as some of the paper was soggy from the dampness of the morning, and would break off and cling to the branches so they had to pluck repeatedly at it to remove it. About fifteen minutes into the job Bylen came out of the house again, carrying a briefcase.

"Deputy," he called out briskly to Jane, who was closest to the house.

"Yes sir?" asked Jane, stopping in her work.

"You and the other deputy will have to move your cars. I can't back mine out to get to work."

Jane didn't react for only a split second, so short a time Bylen in his hurry and self-absorption didn't notice it, then motioned at Galen across the yard. As Galen scurried across the yard Jane got in her patrol car and started it. While she backed out and parked at the curb Galen started his car. He backed out and also parked at the curb across the street. Bylen's Lincoln Town Car appeared out of his garage and he backed swiftly down the driveway. But in the middle of the street he stopped and the driver's side window went down.

"Deputy," he called out to Jane again as she walked back to the yard.

"Yes sir," said Jane professionally, sidetracking to the sleek black car.

"How soon before you find out who the lowlifes are who did this to my lawn?" he asked.

Once again Jane didn't react a split second, which Bylen didn't notice again.

"We'll need some help from you, sir. Who do you know that would have a motive to do this to you?"

Bylen looked completely stunned and snapped back in the leather seat.

"No one I know would have a reason to do this to me! " he declared.

"Then there is very little chance we'll find the vandals who did this, Mr. Bylen," said Jane.

Bylen stewed several seconds in a huff, then the window came up and he drove off, leaving Jane to watch after him, amazed, relieved and annoyed all at the same time, before turning back to the toilet paper in the yard.

It was close to noon when Jane and Galen finally finished the yard. They reported to Mrs. Bylen that the job was done, and she requested that they place the filled bags at the end of the driveway by the curb for the trash men to pick up tomorrow morning. So Jane and Galen had to carry each of the eight bags from where they had filled it on the lawn to the curb.

They drove back down Southview Street and Galen tuned left on Union Drive, the main road into Grangeville on the south side, heading back into town. Jane signaled to turn left too, but had to wait for the traffic. It cleared a few minutes later but before Jane could turn, a car came whipping past her heading out of town and down the road at what had to be ninety miles an hour. She flicked on the flashers and hit the siren and took off after it.

The car, a '65 red Chevy, did not stop nor slow down as Jane pursued it. She hit the accelerator and reached close to ninety herself. As the red Chevy weaved back and forth between the right and left lanes to pass the slower moving cars, Jane weaved back and forth passing them too, only they slowed to the shoulder of the road at the sound of her siren. This allowed her to catch up with the red Chevy and pull up next to it, and signal the driver. The man saw her but continued on several moments, then slowed and drove onto the shoulder too.

Jane parked behind the Chevy and got out of the patrol car, bringing her ticket pad with her. She walked up to the driver's side window and stood next to the windshield, looking in.

The driver slowly rolled down the window. He had an unhappy expression on his face.

"Sir. Do you realize you were going an excess of ninety miles an hour in a forty-five mile zone?" Jane asked him.

The man wagged his head back and forth, looking frustrated now too. He was not much older than Butch, and wore dirty, rough-looking work clothes.

"Yeah, I know I was goin' pretty fast, Officer. But....I'm workin' about twenty miles down the road with a construction crew and I was sent into town to get some pizzas for lunch and I was hurrying back before they got cold," he said.

He spoke in a pleading tone and looked at Jane pleadingly. She looked back at him with no expression several moments, then flipped back the cover of her ticket pad.

"Then I'll write your ticket real fast," she said.

Jane radioed in she was going on her lunch break after she sent the pizza driver on his way, with his ticket. She drove into town and stopped at Uncle Nunzio's herself where she purchased two ham and cheese subs, two bags of potato chips and two Pepsis to go, and continued on to Butch's garage.

Butch was waiting for her this time, and had a place cleared off on his workbench for their lunch. Andy and Pete were setting up their lunches too when Jane came in.

"Hi Janie," said Butch. He kissed her quickly, then took the large white sack from her. Jane sat on the stool in front of the workbench as Butch began to set up their lunch.

"Anything exciting happen this morning Jane?" asked Pete, sitting next to her and eating a peanut butter and jelly sandwich.

"Well, I cleaned up a yard that somebody T.P.ed last night" said Jane, carefully picking up half of her sloppy but delicious sub.

"Somebody got T.P.ed last night?" exclaimed Butch. His eyes widened and glowed with delight. "God, I haven't T.P.ed somebody's lawn in over…" He paused, then spoke casually. "A year and a half." He sighed longingly and straddled his stool and sat on it

"Want us to go T.P. somebody this Devil's Night, Butch?" asked Andy, leaning around Pete and Jane to look at Butch.

Butch glanced at Jane wryly.

"Better not. We do and we'll be the prime suspects to you-know-who-here."

Butch nodded once at Jane, and Andy grinned and nodded as he ate his mother's thick roast beef sandwich.

"That's a smart move, Butch," said Jane, "I'd hate to have to arrest you."

"Would you really throw me in jail, Janie?" asked Butch, before putting a potato chip in his mouth.

"I'm sworn to do my duty, Mr. Przybylski," said Jane. Then she lowered her voice. "But if I had to throw you in jail as a police officer, I'd come later on as your girlfriend and help you break out."

Butch grinned slyly and leaned forward to kiss Jane.

Pete pumped Jane for every single detail when she told him of her high-speed chase with the pizza delivery man. This took up the rest of the lunch hour, and when she finished her lunch and story she kissed Butch good-bye. But he stood up and followed her out to the patrol car.

He had listened to her account of the high speed chase with an interested and amused look on his face, but that expression was gone now and he looked dead serious and concerned, as he followed her out of the garage.

"Butch, you don't have to interrupt your lunch to walk me to the car. I'm a big girl, I can go myself."

Jane reached the car and opened the door. But before she could get in Butch grabbed her wrist to stop her.

"Did you really hit ninety going after that guy?" Butch asked solemnly.

"Yes," said Jane, confused and startled at Butch.

"Damnit. Be careful, will you?" whispered Butch.

Jane continued to look startled at Butch several seconds, then her expression melted into one of happiness and warmth.

"Oh Butch. You mean you'd worry about me?" she said.

"This isn't funny, Janie." He took a step closer to her. "You know I couldn't stand it if something happened to..."

Jane's car radio suddenly crackled to life and Ralph's voice was heard.

"All available patrols. Accident on the comer of Main and Harper Streets," he said.

Jane's attention was torn a second between Butch and answering the call. Then she leaned up and kissed Butch quickly, then reached into the car for the radio microphone.

"Officer Fleming. Reporting to scene," she said into it.

She got into the car and started it, then looked up at Butch. He still was looking at her solemnly.

"I'll see you later. I promise," she said.

Butch's solemn expression left his face as he smiled assuredly.

"You'd better believe it," he said.

The accident happened right in front of the Grangeville Drugstore and Jane's apartment. It involved a battered pickup truck and an equally battered brown Oldsmobile. Each vehicle had one headlight completely smashed and the fender crumpled up all the way to the windshield. The truck's windshield was shattered and pieces of glass lay scattered around both streets. A small crowd of onlookers began to gather and gawk as the two men, obviously the owners and drivers of the vehicles, began to escalate their argument as to who was responsible for the accident.

Jane pulled up across the street and started towards the scene when another patrol car came up and parked behind hers, and Clark got out of it. He said nothing to Jane but dodged the traffic with her that was slowed by the two vehicles blocking the right lane on both Main and Harper Streets. The slowed traffic began to add to the general chaos the scene was beginning to develop, and horns began to blow and words began to be yelled out windows from one driver to another.

"Take it easy now, gentlemen," said Jane, being the first to approach the two men. They were both in their fifties, heavyset, and tough-looking, neither one obviously easygoing, cooperative men. There were aggravated looks, looks getting hotter and hotter as the moments passed, in each of their eyes towards the other. Then they looked at Jane. For a second, the aggravation between themselves seem to redirect itself towards Jane, but then it went back towards its original object and Jane was just a Sheriff's deputy to them.

"What happened here?" asked Clark, coming up then next to Jane.

Both men began to talk at once and nothing could be made out from their words, and their anger began to boil higher. They started to stand up to each other and it looked only a few choice words away before fisticuffs erupted.

"Gentlemen!" Jane spoke firmly and calmly and stepped between the two men, actually forcing them apart The two men calmed a little at the physical separation, but still were breathing fire that needed only a little puff of air to flare up again.

"First of all, we need to get these vehicles off the streets," said Jane.

"I can't even start my car!" bellowed its owner, the man wearing a red and black plaid flannel shirt and a down vest, "This son-of-a-bitch hit it but good!"

"It probably didn't even the hell start before *you* hit *me*," said the truck's owner, also in a plaid flannel shirt but a jacket over it.

"Goddammit, you hit me! " bellowed the car owner.

"Gentlemen! Watch your language! We are in public!" Jane said loudly but calmly. She nodded towards the small knot of people at the opposite curb, a group that was rapidly getting larger and larger. The men glanced over and saw that there were women and young children watching, and the verbal barrage stopped.

"Can you drive your truck?" asked Jane of the truck owner.

"I don't know. Even if I can, I can't see out the window, this jerk hit me so hard it shattered…

"That thing was already cracked bad, I saw it before this blind bat hit me…"

"Do your best, sir," Jane said to the truck owner quickly, before he could answer back to the car owner. He went to the truck and got in, and it did start and he drove it to the closest open parking spot available on Main Street. While he did the car owner tried his vehicle. The engine did not turn over.

"I'll have to call the garage," said Jane. She started for the drugstore to use the pay phone in there, but saw the truck owner walking back. She motioned to Clark.

"Clark, we'd better keep these two apart for awhile. Take him back to his truck and get his account of this," said Jane.

She waited for Clark's answer. But he only shrugged and nodded in agreement. He did not refuse Jane's suggestion. Fifteen minutes after her call Butch drove up in his powerful tow truck. He took in the situation immediately and drove the tow truck in front of the car and positioned it to hook the car up. The car's owner, whose name Jane learned was Stanley Ross from her questioning about his side of the accident, stood on the sidewalk and watched as Butch got out and began hitching up the front of the car to the huge hook of Butch's truck.

"Guess you'll finally have to think seriously about giving up on this old clunker, huh Stan?" said Butch, after securing the car to his truck and looking over at Stan while smiling broadly. Stan looked chagrined at Butch's declaration and didn't watch as Butch got back in the tow truck and started to drive back to his garage. Stan may have wanted to ignore Butch's verdict about his car, but the truck's owner, whose name Clark learned was Wendall Pelon, certainly didn't want to.

"I told you that car was in lousy shape before the accident!" he yelled out from across the street where Clark kept him.

"That's got nothin' to do with you hittin' me!" shouted Stan.

"Gentlemen, as of now the matter is closed. The rest will have to be worked out between your insurance companies," said Jane, loud enough for both of them to hear. "Officer Alfred and I have taken the report, I suggest now you both be on your way."

"And how am I suppose to do that, with my car being towed away?" said Stan.

"I'll take you where you want to go," said Clark, walking across the street after Wendall had left and overhearing Stan's question.

"You will Clark?" said Jane, surprised, "I'll be happy to do it."

"No. You go on, Jane. You go back on patrol. Where do you want to go, Mr. Ross?"

Clark turned his attention to Stan, not letting Jane press the matter further.

"I guess to the Przybylski Garage, to my car," he said.

"Then let's go."

Clark led Stan across the street to his patrol car and they got in, leaving a surprised Jane to watch them leave. Traffic was back to its normal speed, but Jane noticed it was driving over the shattered glass from the truck's front window. She turned and went into the drugstore.

Reese Butterworth was the store's owner, pharmacist and also Jane's landlord, and he was behind the pharmacy counter ringing up a customer's prescription when Jane came in. The customer was just leaving as Jane walked up, and the woman cast Jane a critical eye, but then continued on her departure with no other reaction.

"Mr. Butterworth, can I ask a favor of you?"

Reese Butterworth was a tall, thin man, with white hair and a thin white mustache to go along with the immaculately white pharmacist uniform he always wore at work. He was also a man of strong opinions and especially strong morals, but he was also a realist and as long as Jane paid her rent on time and held no wild swinging parties in her apartment, he never said anything to her about her lifestyle, personal or professional, to her or anybody else. He knew Jane was sleeping with Butch and sometimes in her apartment, but as a drugstore owner Reese knew Jane and Butch were not the only single people in Grangeville who were having sex. Friday and Saturday nights certain embarrassing, but nevertheless real, purchases of a certain personal product were made by the teenage boys of Grangeville. They were the sons of the very same people who came in when he first started renting Jane the apartment above and complained to him about what she was doing up there and he allowing her to do so. He had merely shrugged and said he couldn't be sure what Jane was doing up there with Butch, for all he knew they were playing an all-night Monopoly game.

Reese had heard the crash outside his store that resulted from the Stanley Ross-Wendall Polen accident, and watched a little as Jane handled the situation. When he saw everything was under control he went back to his business.

"What would you like Deputy?" he asked in reply to Jane's question.

"Do you have a broom and pan I may borrow to sweep up the glass outside on the street?" she answered.

"Oh, that's all right, Deputy Fleming," he said, "I have a broom and pan but I'll sweep it up myself."

Jane looked surprised.

"Are you sure, Mr. Butterworth?"

"Of course. I have a responsibility to my place of business and part of it is to make sure the area around it is clean for my customers to get through."

"Well, thank you, Mr. Butterworth," said Jane, still surprised but now pleased.

"No thanks necessary, Deputy Fleming. Just doing my duty. As you do yours."

"Well, good-bye, Mr. Butterworth," said Jane.

"Good-bye Deputy," he replied. And Jane left the store wondering if the run of good luck and cooperation she was getting would continue with Charlie O'Brien, who she was hoping to be able to finally see now.

CHAPTER NINE

Grangeville Junior High was just letting out for the day as Jane drove up to the long white brick building. Smaller than Grangeville Senior High, the junior high was designed similarly, except the main entrance was where the courtyard was in the senior building. Several yellow buses were lined up in front of the entrance in the driveway and students were climbing aboard. A small grip of disappointment took hold of Jane, as she realized she might be too late to find Charlie and talk to him privately. But she parked behind the last bus and started to walk towards the largest congregation of kids.

They eyed her oddly but no one said anything or made a comment. Jane looked around for Charlie but did not pick him out of the group. She was standing next to the open door of the last bus and she took a step towards it.

"Do you drop off a Charlie O'Brien on your route?" she asked the driver.

The driver, a large, tough-looking man in his late sixties, with messy gray hair and five o'clock shadow, glanced down at Jane from his steady gaze at the mirror over his head which allowed him to see his passengers' actions. He had just barked out an order for some boisterous young person to sit down on his seat, not stand on it, and when he looked down at Jane his face was in a very annoyed scowl.

"I don't get to know 'em, I just haul 'em back and forth to school, lady," he said. Then Jane's uniform registered on him and his scowl changed to surprise and respect. "I mean, Deputy," he added, with regard.

"You are looking for Charles O'Brien?" said a voice behind and to the left of Jane. She turned around and before her stood a skinny, blond-haired young man with dark rimmed glasses and not a little acne on his face. He carried a briefcase and a row of pencils lined his white shirt breast pocket, the pocket protected from the lead of the pencils by a plastic holder. The boy's expression was serious and formal.

"Yes I am. Do you happen to know which bus he takes?" asked Jane.

"Charles doesn't take a bus. He rides his bicycle to and from school. You will find him on the other side of the parking lot close to the back of the school. That's where the bicycle rack is."

"Thank you," said Jane, impressed at the boy's demeanor as well as a little amazed. So much so she was moved to find out who he was. "And what's your name?"

"Russell McCafferty Brown," he stated.

"I'm Deputy Jane Fleming," she said. "Nice to meet you Russell. And thanks again for your help."

"You're welcome." Jane started to walk off but then Russell spoke up again.

Jane stopped and looked at him, as students continued to pass each of them and climb on the bus.

"Yes Russell?"

Russell paused a little as he appeared to be a little unsure of himself, then regained his poise.

"Let me just say I'm behind the women's movement one hundred percent and the statement you are making by pursuing your goal to be an active law enforcement officer," he said stoutly.

Jane looked at him amazed yet sincere a moment

"Well, thank you Russell. That's nice to know."

Russell nodded once in return, then mounted the steps and entered the bus.

Russell's information was correct as Jane walked down the parking lot and approached the back of the school. A long bike rack stood next to the sidewalk Jane walked down and several students were packing their bikes with their books and other beings preparing to leave. Jane spotted Charlie O'Brien right away. He was strapping a stack of books onto the back of a ten-speed and didn't see Jane as she walked right up to him.

"Charlie. Can I talk to you a minute?" she said.

Charlie's head jerked up startled, but immediately looked panicked when he saw who it was. From the amount of panic in him Jane realized

Charlie would have the weakest resistance of anyone to whom she had talked to any pressure she might put on him by her questions. If she was going to get something substantial out of anyone, it was Charlie O'Brien

"What do you want?" he asked, panicked. Jane also saw that his panicked state paralyzed him, as he stood like a stone next to his bike.

"I want to talk to you about your sister," said Jane, lowering her voice so the other students won't hear. But the students were swiftly leaving them alone at the bike rack as they climbed aboard and began pedaling off. Soon Jane and Charlie were completely alone at the back of the school and on the farthest side of the parking lot from the driveway.

"What about my sister? Did you find her?" Charlie asked.

"No. But I hope to soon. If you'll help me," said Jane.

"I don't know nothing about Jennie being gone," declared Charlie, a little defiance stirring up in him.

"Charlie, I think you do," declared Jane. The panic took over Charlie again.

"I don't," he said.

"Charlie, how did you and your sister get along?"

Charlie looked startled at this sudden shift of subject.

"How'd we get along?" said Charlie.

"Were you close? Did you and your sister confide in each other?"

"Yeah, well, we talked, about…things," said Charlie, relaxing quite a bit now, thrown off the panic track by the unusualness of the questions.

"Things like, how Jennie felt about Steve?"

"Oh yeah. Lots about how Jennie felt about Steve."

"Real personal things about how she felt about Steve?"

"Yeah."

Jane looked at Charlie closely. There was still enough residual panic in him so he was susceptible to enough pressure that would make him break down. This was what Jane was aiming for: Charlie being comfortable enough to talk but panicked enough not to be able to resist her.

"Charlie, were Jennie and Steve sleeping together?" Jane asked quietly.

Charlie looked down at the sidewalk several seconds before he spoke. "Yeah. They were. They did."

"Jennie tell you this?"

Charlie shook his head. "No. I found them. I...my folks were going to be gone all day one Saturday, to Marcellus, and I was gonna spend the night at my friend Nick's house. I forgot my baseball glove and I went home to get it. When I went upstairs to my room I heard...I heard noises coming from Jennie's room and I opened the door and...and...I saw them, in Jennie's bed, together." Charlie now dropped his head and studies his shoes. "I ran downstairs and Steve came after me and then Jennie. She begged me not to tell our folks, and Steve promised I could drive his car if I wouldn't. So..." Charlie's tone lightened. "I didn't. And I got to drive Steve's car."

Charlie remained staring at his shoes but it appeared he was relieved to have finally told that story.

"When did this happen Charlie?" Jane asked quietly.

"About a month ago."

"September?"

"Yeah."

Jane shifted on her feet and looked down at her own shoes.

"Charlie, did Jennie and Steve use...birth control?"

Charlie's head jerked up so fast his hair flipped away from his forehead. He looked at Jane wide-eyed and now something beyond panic took hold of him.

"I don't know anything about that! I don't know anything!" Charlie suddenly found his limbs and he backed his bike away from the rack and jumped on it. Without a glance at Jane he started pedaling furiously away from her, but Jane did not try to stop him nor call him back. Charlie had told her enough.

Now there was only one more person Jane wanted to talk to, and the last one she knew she would need to...Steve Ballard. Figuring since the junior high had already let out the senior high would be too and Steve would be home, Jane drove over to the Ballard residence a third time.

But Steve wasn't there. Mrs. Ballard came to the door at the sound of the bell.

"Yes Deputy" she asked, with no noticeable annoyance towards Jane's repeat appearance.

"May I speak to your son, Mrs. Ballard?" said Jane.

"Oh, he's not here. He's at football practice. He's still at school."

"Oh, well, thank you." Jane turned to walk off but then stepped back to Mrs. Ballard. "Did you find the sweater Steve was wearing the night Jennie disappeared Mrs. Ballard?"

"No. I haven't," she replied, truly puzzled, "I'll have to ask Steve about it."

"You'll let me know what he says," said Jane, just before she left.

Jane could see the Grangeville football team in practice on the field as she drove up to the high school. Parking on the driveway closest to the football field, she walked through the entrance gate and towards the small group of adults standing by the benches. One of them happened to glance behind himself and saw Jane approaching. He nudged the taller man next to him and motioned towards Jane. The taller man turned from watching the practice and saw Jane too, just as she came up to him.

"Can I do something for you, Officer?" he asked.

"I'm Deputy Jane Fleming," she said, offering her hand.

"I had a hunch," said the taller man with a friendly half-grin. He shook Jane's hand. "Donald Warneke. Coach of the Grangeville High Falcons football team."

Warneke was an extremely, strikingly handsome man in his early fifties, with salt and pepper hair and strong, manly features. He had blue eyes and a ruddy complexion darkened by a suntan, and in the back of Jane's mind she imagined this was what Butch would look like when he got older. Warneke had on a cap with "Grangeville Falcons" embossed on it and a dark blue windbreaker with "Coach" embossed on it on the left front.

"I'd like to talk to one of your players, Coach Warneke, if it won't disrupt your practice too much," said Jane.

"Steve Ballard?" he offered.

Jane looked a little surprised. "Yes," she replied.

"No problem. I was planning on taking a break soon anyway." Warneke turned out to the players scrimmaging on the field. "Okay guys! Time out! Take a break!" he shouted out at them. The boys broke up and started trotting towards the benches. "Ballard! You come over here!" Warneke added.

One of the helmeted players broke away from the group and trotted over to the coach. He removed his helmet as he reached him and Jane saw it was Steve, and when he saw her, as she had been standing behind the coach and his assistant, and didn't see her earlier, his expression went stone cold.

"Deputy Fleming would like to talk to you," said Warneke, in a tone that had an order shade to it as well. Steve's glance went between Warneke and Jane several times, as if torn between obedience to his coach and not wanting to have a thing to do with Jane. But Jane didn't give him a chance to decide against her.

"Why don't we step over here a ways so we can talk in private?" said Jane.

She started walking towards the fifty yard line and Steve followed, albeit reluctantly. When they reached mid-field they stopped.

"What's so important you gotta talk to me about that you come interrupt my football practice?" said Steve a touch angrily, shifting his helmet which he had resting on his hip and supported by his arm.

"Your girlfriend, Steve," said Jane solemnly, "She's been missing almost a week. I would think you'd feel nothing was more important than that."

Steve said nothing but glanced away, once again his expression cold.

"Steve, what time did you and Jennie go up to Pebble Creek?" asked Jane, ignoring Steve's reaction.

"Seven-thirty," he said, mumbling it.

"What time?" asked Jane, even though she had heard it.

"Seven-thirty," Steve said stoutly, snapping his head towards her.

"And how long were you up there before you had the argument about Jennie wanting to date other guys and she ran off?" asked Jane.

Steve's expression turned into a puzzled one, and was also a little taken aback.

"Ah, I don't know," Steve said, shrugging. Now he seemed unconcerned. "Fifteen minutes," he said.

"Okay. And your mother tells me you got home at nine-thirty. What happened during that hour and forty-five minutes?"

"I told you earlier," said Steve, now getting angry, "I was mad, too. I drove around till I cooled off."

"Almost two hours to cool off. You must have a hot temper," said Jane.

That temper was evident now in Steve's whole being. Jane could see his chest rising up and down swiftly.

"Steve, I've talked with Jennie's mother and Jennie's girlfriends and they all told me Jennie was completely in love with you. And that she never told any of them that she wanted to date any other guys. And if that's true why would you and she have an argument about that?"

"Are you trying to call me a liar?" shouted Steve, dropping his helmet and looming over Jane. His voice carried over the football field and Coach Warneke and his assistants and the players all looked over at him and Jane.

"I'm trying to find the truth about your girlfriend's disappearance Steve," said Jane, holding her ground and her voice calm. She looked at him straight in the eye several moments. "Steve, Charlie told me what happened that one Saturday last month. About how he found you and Jennie in her bed together."

Her words were the last things that registered to Jane before everything suddenly going black. Then the next thing she knew she smelled an excruciatingly strong scent, then realized she was flat on her back. One by one other things registered: something was wet on her nose and around her mouth and the back of her head hurt. But that pain was nothing to the throbbing agony that was suppose to be her nose. She opened her eyes slowly to see Coach Warneke holding smelling salts in her face and a shocked and concerned expression on his. She registered noises now and she heard a male juvenile voice call out: "Christ, Steve, ya hit a cop!"

"Don't move Deputy," said Coach Warneke, as Jane tried to sit up.

"I'm all right," insisted Jane, sitting up. When she did the world began to spin around her and the crowd surrounding her and Warneke became a mass of faces and bodies. She grabbed at Warneke's arm and held it till the spinning stopped.

"Brian, go call an ambulance," Warneke said to his assistant standing next to him.

"No! no, that's not necessary, I'm fine," said Jane. Everything was back to normal now except for the throbbing which was in her nose, she now realized. She struggled to stand and with Warneke's help she did. Around her now she saw the players of the Grangeville football team and the rest of Warneke's assistants, all staring at her. Jane swallowed and she tasted something bitter in her mouth that normally wasn't there, and when she put her hand up to her face and wiped it, saw when she drew her hand away a large amount of blood on her fingers.

"Deputy, you could be seriously hurt. You might have a concussion. Now we got to get you to the hospital," said Warneke firmly.

"Was I hit that hard?" asked Jane, looking directly at him.

"Steve…is a very strong young man," Warneke said.

"Where is Steve?" asked Jane, looking around.

"I sent him back to the locker room. Deputy, I know you have every right to arrest him for striking you, but, as his coach, and his friend, would you let it pass? Steve hasn't been himself lately. He normally wouldn't do anything like this. He's a good kid. A real good kid. Do you think you could just let this go?"

Jane tried to take a deep breath but nothing came in through her nose so she had to take one through her mouth. Then she nodded.

"Okay Coach. I won't arrest Steve." She paused. "He's already in big enough trouble as it is."

Coach Warneke, and what seemed like every member of the Grangeville football team, helped Jane to the benches where they sat her down and waited for the ambulance to arrive. With sirens blaring and flashers swirling, it drove up on the football field to where Jane sat fifteen minutes later. Once again it seemed everyone there had a hand in getting Jane on the stretcher and into the ambulance. Again with sirens and flashers the vehicle took Jane to Grangeville General Hospital.

Still strapped to the stretcher and her head positioned to stop her throbbing nose from bleeding, Jane was wheeled into the emergency room where the staff, notified in advance by the ambulance driver that he was bringing in a Sheriff's deputy, converged on her en masse. She was wheeled into a separate room, transferred to a gurney, had her holster removed and shirt sleeve rolled up so a nurse could take her blood pressure while a doctor took her pulse, then listened to her heartbeat. He then checked the reaction of her eyes with a penlight, and made her follow his fingers with them.

"Nose hurts pretty good, I'll bet," the doctor said. His nametag said "Dr. R. Ekert, M.D." "We'll take care of that," he added, and while the nurse began washing the blood off Jane's face the doctor reached into a nearby cabinet and brought out a hypodermic needle and a small bottle. He filled the needle, then had Jane roll to her side. The nurse unzipped Jane's pants so the doctor could pull them down and jab the needle into Jane's rear. She made a quick intake of breath but no other sound.

"Okay, send her up to X-ray, let's get some pictures of her head," he said. He was a tall, somewhat comical-looking man with a large fleshy nose and rounded chin, wearing a stark white doctor's coat. But he was both businesslike and reassuring in his dealing with Jane and he patted her on the shoulder gently as Jane was wheeled out of the room and over to the X-ray department.

No sooner was Jane positioned on the table and the X-ray technician moved in position behind a window to take the X-rays than a commotion was heard down the hallway and voices all speaking at once. The words could not be made out nor who exactly was talking, but the tone and inflection of one of them ignited a spark of recognition in Jane and she gasped. The technician noticed Jane's reaction and then heard the voices in the hallway. One seemed to be getting closer and suddenly Butch was in the room.

"Janie, all you all right?" he said frantically.

He ran right up next to where Jane was laying on the table and the X-ray machine was poised over her face. Butch's expression was as frantic as his tone and his face was flushed red. He was wearing an old pair of jeans, a flannel shirt with his oldest, most battered sweater vest over it, and his most beat-up pair of tennis shoes. He looked a ragged sight.

"Butch!" said Jane, startled to see him but deep down also happy and pleased he had showed up. She could only turn her head slightly towards him as the X-ray machine loomed extremely close to her face.

The technician and a stout nurse both came up to the table where Jane lay at the same time. The technician looked confused but the nurse was livid, at Butch.

"Young man! You must leave here immediately!" she declared more than just a little firmly.

"The hell I will! I'm staying right here!" Butch snapped just as firmly at the nurse.

"Young man, don't make me call security!" said the nurse.

"Mister, if you stay here you're going to expose yourself to unnecessary radiation," said the technician.

"If Jane's gonna be exposed to it, so will I," declared Butch.

"Oh Butch," said Jane warmly and under her breath. But as much as she would have liked Butch to continue standing there and hold her hand, as he had done the moment he reached her, practicality took her over.

"It's all right Butch. Go wait outside. I'll be all right," she said to him.

"We won't be long," said the technician.

Butch was seen to reluctantly give in and he walked out, but not before he kissed Jane's hand gently before letting it go.

The technician took four pictures of Jane's head: front, back, and both sides.

When he finished, Jane was wheeled back to the emergency room area and the small section she was in before. Butch was in there waiting for her, alone.

"Didn't I just tell you this afternoon to be careful? And didn't you promise me you would?" said Butch angrily, but the worry in his eyes nullified it. He sat on the edge of the gurney and took Jane's hand again.

"Yes," said Jane, lying back on the gurney and turning her head to see Butch easier.

"Well, what the hell happened?" said Butch, less angry now but still worried.

"My nose ran into somebody's fist," said Jane, and she grinned.

Butch looked perturbed at her answer but also amused.

"How did you find out about me?" Jane asked.

"Pete called me at home. I decided to do a little fishing this afternoon so I left work a little early to be ready when you got off. I had everything ready and supper packed to take with us and then Pete called me and said they had taken you to the hospital."

"How did Pete find out?" asked Jane curiously.

"I didn't ask him. Who knows? I told you news shoots through this town like greased lightening," replied Butch, "And when I asked Pete why you were in the hospital, he didn't know so I got in the car and drove right over here." Butch motioned with his head out the door. "Then I get here and the daughter of Dr. Frankenstein didn't want me going back to you. And she said she couldn't tell me what was wrong with you. Something about only close relatives."

"I'm sorry you were so worried about me Butch," said Jane, touched by the anguish in Butch's words.

Butch gave a small sly grin, now completely relieved seeing Jane alive and reasonable in one piece.

"My pleasure, Ma'am," he whispered, "There's no one else I'd rather worry about.

"Thank you," whispered Jane, just before hers and Butch's lips met gently when Butch lowered his head to hers.

"How's your nose feel?" Butch asked, raising his lips just an inch.

"Like it's about the size of a hot-air balloon," said Jane.

"But it's a lovely shade of red," said Butch.

They were still kissing when Dr. Ekert came in, and he cleared his throat heavily to let them know he was there. Butch and Jane broke off the kiss and looked at the doctor standing in the doorway.

"You are a very lucky young woman, Deputy," said Dr. Ekert. He was holding Jane's X-rays and he held one up to the light when he stood by Jane's gurney. "There's no sign of a concussion, and your nose is not broken. It'll be a little red and swollen for a few days, but an ice pack on it occasionally will help that. And a couple of aspirin should take care of any discomfort."

"How long should she take off work?" asked Butch.

"To be honest, if she just gets a good night's sleep tonight, there's no reason why she couldn't go back to work tomorrow as usual."

"Can I go with Butch fishing, Doctor?" asked Jane.

"You're crazy. Forget the fishing," said Butch.

"But you were planning on it, Butch. And I'd like to go," said Jane.

"Actually a nice round of fishing is the best way to relax I can think of. Go. And enjoy yourself. Just don't try to land a Marlin," said Dr. Ekert.

"Thank you, Doctor," said Jane.

"Take care, Deputy. I've signed your release papers and a nurse will be by soon to wheel you out. Good-bye."

"Good-bye, Doctor," said Jane.

"Bye, Doc," said Butch, as the doctor left the room.

"Where'd they put my gun?" Jane asked Butch, when he helped her sit up and she started to straighten her clothes. Butch looked around the room and spotted the holster hanging on the hook on the back of the door.

"Here it is," he said. He picked it off and handed it to Jane.

"I'll go bring the car around and wait for you by the exit," he said, as Jane strapped her holster on.

"That's not necessary, Butch. I can walk to the car," said Jane.

"Indulge me on this, Wonder Woman. Let me at least do this little thing to accommodate your injury," he said, in a tone that said he would take no argument.

"All right," said Jane good-naturedly.

Butch left the room and Jane was alone several minutes. She finished straightening her clothes and as she was readjusting her holster she heard footsteps and looked up, expecting the nurse. Instead, it was Ralph who walked in.

Jane would not have been as surprised to see Ralph had he not had the expression on his face that he did. He looked startled, amazed, confused and concerned all at once. Ralph stopped at the doorway and stood looking at Jane several moments.

Ralph was now seeing Jane with a slightly different view. Still she was his first female deputy and still that fact irritated him, but now, she was also his first deputy ever to be injured. In the line of duty or on off-hours. Never before had a member of the Grangeville Sheriff's Department ever been hurt enough that hospitalization was needed. As Ralph continued to stare Jane became puzzled herself.

"Sheriff?" she asked curiously.

Ralph snapped out of his gaze and his head jerked up.

"Deputy. How are you?" he asked.

"I'm...all right, Sheriff," said Jane, and she gave a small smile.

"What happened?" asked Ralph, walking into the room and up next to the gurney, "I was told you were struck in the face and were rushed to the emergency room." He looked her face over.

"Steve Ballard didn't like what I said to him."

"Steve Ballard?" repeated Ralph, "What did you say?"

Jane paused a moment to prepare a careful answer.

"Something personal. And this was his reaction to it." And Jane motioned to her nose.

"I'll have him arrested right away," said Ralph.

"No. Please, Sheriff. Don't arrest him. I don't wish to see him arrested...now. I told his coach I would let it pass."

Ralph was sure of Jane's conviction but not sure of her motive for it. But he didn't press her about it.

"Well, take the rest of the day off, and the week, for that matter, to recuperate."

"Thank you, Sheriff. I'd like the rest of the day, but the doctor said the week's not necessary. I'll be at work tomorrow."

Ralph again looked amazed.

"Very well, Deputy," he said. The firm look on Jane's face had a shade of her well-known-to-Ralph determination in it and he didn't feel like fighting her about this either, not in her injured state.

"Butch is here to pick me up, and I will have him take me back to the high school to drive back the patrol car," said Jane.

"Never mind Deputy," said Ralph, "I'll have Clark and Galen go pick up your patrol car. You just go home now and rest."

Before Jane could argue a nurse came in pushing a wheelchair. Jane started to slide off the gurney and to her surprise Ralph grabbed her arm helpfully as she did. He kept hold of her arm as she sat on the wheelchair and the nurse helped her arrange her feet on the foot stands, not letting go till she was completely comfortable and secure on it.

"Thank you for showing up, Sheriff," said Jane.

Ralph shifted a little uncomfortably under Jane's warm smile.

"It's necessary, Deputy. I need the hospital report for the department's records."

Jane knew this was true, but Ralph didn't have to come see her too, so she dismissed the phlegmatic tone of his voice and smiled anyway. The nurse wheeled Jane around and pushed her out the door as Ralph remained and watched them leave.

Jane and the nurse had to pass the emergency room waiting area on the way to the exit, and when Jane made a casual glance into it, she was surprised to see Tim Usher in there. He was standing with his hands behind his back, and an odd expression on his face as he stared unseeing in front of him.

"Tim?" she called out.

The nurse stopped when Jane spoke. Tim's head jerked up and he looked in her direction. His odd expression changed to one of relief, and he smiled as he walked over to her.

"What are you doing here?" Jane asked.

"I heard one of Grangeville's finest was brought to the hospital emergency room over the police band, and I came right over to cover the story," he said.

"Oh. Well, there's really not much of a story," said Jane, slightly chagrined.

"Why don't you tell me what happened, and let me decide," said Tim, "I'm the newspaperman here."

So Jane went into a thorough but brief description of what happened, but didn't notice that Tim simply stood there and smiled and didn't take any notes.

"The doctor said I'm fine, my nose isn't broken and I don't have a concussion. And, I'll be able to go to work tomorrow," she concluded.

"Thank goodness," said Tim. Then to her surprise, he leaned down and kissed her, very briefly but very firmly, on the mouth.

"Do you have a way home?" he then asked, as Jane stared at him speechless for a few seconds.

"Ah, yes, Butch is waiting for me outside," she said finally.

"Oh," said Tim, though he didn't sound very surprised, "Well, I won't keep you from him any longer."

"Good-bye," said Jane, as the nurse began pushing her again towards the glass double doors that were the exit.

"Take care, Deputy," replied Tim after her.

***

Butch had discovered a small, secluded clearing from which to fish in the woods around the Dowagiac River about three miles from where the river came closest to Grangeville, which was Pops Griffiths' store. Here he and Jane were in the next to the last rays of the Indian Summer afternoon sun an hour after she was released from the hospital The clearing was surrounded by the thick forest of Pebble Creek's most remote section, the north section, and was close enough to the river so Butch could sit and hold his fishing rod out over the river while in his customary position; sitting cradled between Jane's legs as she sat behind him on the thick picnic blanket, his head resting on her chest.

The quiet, lazy times of Butch fishing in the Dowagiac were always some of Jane's favorites with him, and this clearing was one of her favorite places to be. Whatever troubles, pressures or hassles she experienced vanished when she was here, with Butch resting between her raised knees and her fingers fiddling with his hair. This time she forgot the problem of whether to tell Butch about Tim's innocent kiss. She dismissed it as just that, a kiss between good friends after a moment of anxiety.

She and Butch had settled in the clearing and ate the picnic supper Butch put together, then assumed their regular positions so Butch could begin fishing. They sat quite awhile without Butch getting so much as a nibble on his line, so he opened the copy of the Chronicle he bought and read aloud Tim's account of the softball game.

"Man's a damn good sportswriter," said Butch, when he was finished. Then he finished the can of beer in his hand.

"Want another, sweetheart?" Jane asked, reaching towards the small wicker picnic basket next to her as she did.

"No," said Butch emphatically, "I feel like I'm going to be floating away any minute already."

Jane grinned and caressed a curl of his hair that stood up next to his ear. Having to always watch how she reacted to Butch physically when around other people or possibly being seen by other people, when they were completely alone like this she was moved to indulge in touching him in intimate and loving ways. It was the spot that brought out the feeling and impulse in her, she decided. What was glorious about it too was not only

did she like to do it, but Butch had told her he liked it, which in this place
had sent her heart soaring. Butch sighed contentedly as Jane continued to
stroke his hair, but a few moments later his eyes widened.

"Ooops. I'm starting to drift now. Here. Hold this." He handed Jane
his fishing rod and got up. "I'll be right back."

Jane held the rod and smiled after Butch as he ground out, with the
heel of his tennis shoe, the cigar he had been smoking and disappeared
into the brush downstream.

"Watch out for poison ivy," she called out to him.

"Very funny," came back to her. Jane grinned.

When Butch finished his necessary activity, he turned to walk back up
the riverbank, but he caught sight of something unusual out of the corner
of his eye and he stopped to look in that direction. He was at the point of
the river where the rapids began, where several rocks jutted up in the middle of the river, large rocks with sharp points on them. It was on one of
these sharp points that what caught Butch's eye was held.

Jane was lifting the rod up to check the bait when she heard Butch's
voice call out to her.

"Janie!" to yelled, "Janie, come here!"

Jane dropped the fishing rod and scrambled to her feet, the urgency in
Butch's voice prompting her to quickness. She ran through the brush
where Butch had and a moment later spotted him standing down river,
staring out to the middle of it.

"What is it Butch?" she asked, running up and stopping next to him.

"Look," he said, pointing at a rock in the middle of the river. Jane
looked where he pointed.

Waving up and down in the water's current while caught on the sharp
point of the rock, was a large blue cloth with what appeared to be fringes
on the edge. Jane glanced up at Butch in surprise and then took a step
towards the river. But Butch stopped her.

"Wait. I'll go. The current's too strong here for you."

Before she could argue he stepped into the water and began wading towards the rock.

"Be careful Butch," said Jane.

"Yes Mother," he replied. But he did sway a second later under the current and almost fell. Jane jumped forwards to go to his aid but Butch caught himself and continued on. He reached the rock and pulled the cloth off, struggling with it because of its saturation with water. Flinging it over his shoulder he waded back to the bank.

Jane helped him pull the heavy cloth off his shoulder. It was so heavy Butch was sagging to one side. The cloth landed with a splat on the ground. Jane knelt on one knee to examine it.

"What's it look like to you?" she asked, but with a knowing look on her face.

"Looks like a spread that belongs on somebody's bed," said Butch knowingly.

***

Ralph was at the front desk when Butch and Jane came in with the sodden bedspread. Butch had it over his shoulder again, but with it folded up in a neater fashion it was easier for him to manage. It was still soaked with water and it dropped on the floor behind and in front of Butch. Ralph looked up at their entrance and watched in amazed puzzlement as Butch pulled the sopping mass off his shoulder and dumped it on the desk.

"What is this?" asked Ralph. The concern he had felt earlier towards Jane was totally covered by the embarrassment he felt now by being in her presence along with the man she slept with. To see Jane actually with the man she had illicit sex with made Ralph even more uncomfortable than he regularly did, and now afraid too he would inadvertently say something about it and really cause himself embarrassment. But Jane was too caught up with her and Butch's find to notice. Butch was not, though.

"I think it's the bedspread missing from Pops' bed, Sheriff," said Jane. Ralph winced inwards at the word "bed," it emphasized the fact Butch and Jane slept together all afresh in his mind. He cleared his throat and looked at the cloth, not seeing Butch step back and eye him, while taking a box of small cigars out of the dry side of his sweater, take one and light it. Though looking at the cloth Ralph could sense Butch watching him, very amused.

"What makes you think that?" asked Ralph.

"What makes me think that?" asked Jane, both surprised and annoyed. Perhaps Ralph wasn't as prepared to hear her theory regarding Jennie's disappearance and Pops' murder as she had thought earlier. Jane got hold of herself. "That's what it is," she began calmly, "A bedspread. Look at it." Jane lifted part of it slightly and it sloshed water all around the desk. Ralph moved back slightly. What else could it be? And there was a bedspread missing from Pops' bedroom."

"Where did you find this?" asked Ralph.

"Butch found it in the Dowagiac. We were fishing nearby."

Ralph found himself glancing at Butch with those words, a glance that was totally spontaneous and not consciously directed at all, but done nevertheless. Butch was staring at Ralph with that all-knowing expression. Ralph found it unnerving the way Butch seemed to be able to look inside someone's head and know what they were thinking. Ralph knew Butch all of Butch's life, and had first noticed he could do this when he was a teenager, but Ralph suspected Butch could always do this. Butch folded one arm over his chest while propping the other one on it to smoke his cigar. He drew the cigar away after taking a puff and grinned at Ralph, the smoke trailing out of his mouth slightly. Ralph pulled his eyes away from Butch and back to Jane.

"Now you know Pops' store is only a few hundred yards from the river. It could easily have been taken there and thrown in," said Jane.

"True," said Ralph. Jane looked startled at his agreement with her, and was actually speechless for a few seconds. But the reason for her speechlessness changed with Ralph's next words. "But, why?"

"Why would it be taken off the bed and all the way to the river and thrown in? For what reason?" Ralph went on. He shook his head vigorously. "Look, we don't even know if this belongs to Pops, if it really is his missing spread."

"Well, why don't you try and find out?" asked Butch suddenly, seriously, "You don't have any other leads to follow, do you?"

For a split second during his words Butch's expression was serious too. Then his wicked all-knowing one returned when he finished speaking and he puffed on his cigar again. Ralph was now the speechless one while Jane found her voice.

"See if Forensics can do something to find out if its Pops' or not," said Jane. Ralph looked at her at her words.

"All, right," he said finally.

"Thank you Sheriff," said Jane, releasing a deep sigh. She turned and started out. Butch paused a split second to stare at Ralph, then followed her. Ralph sighed himself in exasperation after him, then looked even more exasperated as he stared at the soggy mess of material sitting, dripping, on the desk.

***

It was after two o'clock in the morning when the phone rang next to the bed, where Jane slept in Butch's protective arms. He had taken Jane in hand the minute they got back home from fishing and delivering the bedspread to Ralph. He ran a hot bath filled with Epsom salts for her to soak in while he prepared some hot chocolate for her and himself. Then he sat next to her on the sofa so she could cuddle up beside him as they drank the chocolate and watched some television and Jane, in her big, warm, white terry cloth robe, alternated drinking the chocolate with holding the ice pack Butch prepared for her to her nose. After the eleven o'clock news Butch put Jane to bed, then got in close next to her.

Butch stirred first, the phone being on the nightstand next to his side of the bed, and tried to roll away from Jane and remove his arms from around her without waking her. But as the phone continued to ring Jane did awaken and watched in the faint light as Butch turned over to answer the phone, sighing disgusted as he did.

"Hello, and who the hell is this?" he said sternly. He laid back on his back, closed his eyes and rubbed his face as he listened. Then he looked surprised, and completely angry. "What in the hell are you doing calling here at this time of the night?" he said. Again he listened, and scowled. "Is it important? It damn well better be." He sighed as he got his answer. "All right." He turned to Jane and held the receiver out to her. "It's for you," he said.

Jane looked curious as well as sleepy and took the phone.

"Who is it?" she whispered.

"One of your fellow deputies. Clark," said Butch, slightly contemptuously.

Butch's answer stunned Jane fully awake and she held the receiver to her head.

"Hello?" Jane said. Butch watched her as she listened, her expression suddenly going blank. She listened for a few more moments, her expression remaining blank. "Yes. I'd want to know. Thank you. Good-bye."

She handed the receiver back to Butch and he hung it up.

"What did Clark call for?" Butch asked.

Jane swallowed.

"To tell me Jennie O'Brien's been found," she said, her blank expression changing towards a solemn one.

"Where?"

"Outside of Niles. She's...she's dead, Butch."

Butch and Jane looked at each other solemnly for several moments in the dimness.

"You knew she was dead, didn't you? Before the call," said Butch finally, "Even earlier."

Jane nodded.

"You know, you never did tell me how you thought Pops' murder and Jennie's disappearance were connected," said Butch, "Why don't you tell me now?"

CHAPTER TEN

An even blacker overcast hung over Grangeville the next day, although the Indian Summer sun shone just as brightly and warmly as it had five days ago at the news of Pops' death. The news of Jennie O'Brien being found dead flew through the town like a whirlwind, also like Pops' death. The combination of the two tragedies virtually paralyzed the townspeople. But the memorial for Pops was to go on as usual, and now include Jennie Mary O'Brien in the services.

Jane, Clark, Galen and the other deputies of the morning shift were gathered in the Sheriff's office before heading for the high school football field and the memorial. Ralph came out of his office carrying the clipboard with the official report on Jennie's death. At his appearance the low talk between the deputies stopped and they all looked at him.

"All right. Here it is. The preliminary report on the O'Brien girl," he said. He looked down on the clipboard. "Caucasian female, approximately 15 to 20 years old, discovered on the banks of the Dowagiac River just outside of Niles, Michigan by two juvenile males at approximately nine-thirty last night. Female was half-clothed. Dead approximately five days, cause of death…" Ralph paused and sighed. "Loss of blood."

Jane's eyes widened at Ralph's last words.

"'Loss of blood?' Is that all it says, Sheriff?"

"That's the preliminary report. The autopsy will determine the reason for the loss of blood."

Ralph sighed again and flipped back the paper on his clipboard.

"Okay. Let's move out. Galen, you and Deputy Fleming will handle the traffic at the high school, the rest of you," Ralph looked over at the other deputies, "Are assigned to security during the service. Let's go." And they all left, Galen pouting at both being assigned to traffic and being called only "Galen" again.

As Jane drove to the high school she fumed at what the report on Jennie said about her death. True, it was only a preliminary report, and when the autopsy was done the full explanation would be known, but even then, the explanation would need an explanation. It seemed to Jane despite all the pieces of information she had put together, she was still too far away from being able to state unequivocally what she knew happened to Jennie O'Brien. What she decided she needed was real evidence, tangible evidence, to finally be able to do that. The discovery of the bedspread yesterday gave her an idea to follow through to find that evidence after she was finished at the memorial.

Main Street was deserted when, close to noon, the time when the memorial was scheduled to start, a red convertible Porsche came down it. The driver slowed down the considerable speed the car was traveling when she noticed the absence of people on the street. As the car passed the Przybylski Garage a faint clanking sound came from inside, the only indication of life in what the driver felt was a hick town.

The sound from the garage came from Butch, alone and working on a '69 Chevy. He was just straightening up from leaning into the car's motor when he heard an impatient horn of an automobile out on the street in front of the garage. He had given Andy and Pete the afternoon off to attend the memorial for Pops, which they felt obligated to do for their mothers' sakes since they held Pops in such high regard, but Butch didn't expect too much business during the memorial anyway so he let them go. He was prepared to interrupt his work if someone did stop by for gas, but the sound of the horn wasn't coming from the pump area, so this had nothing to do with someone needing gas for their car. To Butch's mechanic's ear it was not the horn of an American made automobile. That fact piqued his curiosity, since no one in Grangeville owned a foreign car. It had to be a stranger. But the impatient sound of the horn piqued his annoyance, so though Butch hadn't even met this stranger yet, already he didn't like him.

As the horn persisted, getting more and more inpatient, Butch scowled slightly and tossed the wrench he was using on the workbench. Taking the rag from his back hip uniform pocket he wiped his hands on it as he walked to the front of the garage.

The driver was leaning down looking in the glove compartment as Butch left the garage and started to walk up to the car where it was parked next to the curb. So this person didn't even have the courtesy to drive up into the station, he expected whoever to come out and make a special trip for him. Butch's annoyance with the driver grew, but was moved aside from his full attention after he took the car in with one sweeping glance, admiring only the second Porsche he had ever seen in his life. Then his look was drawn to the driver as the driver sat up away from the glove compartment. His look lost the admiring expression and annoyance took over again.

The driver was a woman. And where Butch lost the admiring expression on his face, the woman picked it up. She eyed Butch approvingly but also lasciviously. A corner of her carefully made-up mouth went up in a half smile.

"I'm Sylvia Griffiths," she said in a soft, slightly husky voice.

Butch's expression remained annoyed, unimpressed by anything about the woman, except the arrogance she showed by the lack of greeting to him and only introduced herself instead. To an outside eye she was a beautiful woman. Her blonde hair was short, highlighted, and carefully and obviously expensively coiffed, still in place despite the top being down on her car. The rest of her make-up was as skillfully and flatteringly applied as her lipstick, and her nails were long, bright red and highly manicured. Her clothes were high fashion and indicated a good figure in spite of her position of sitting in the car. But Butch noticed none of this, only that she had not said hello first but declared her identity first, as if he really might give a damn who this impatient and annoying person was and be impressed by it. If there was anything Butch hated most it was an egotist, and this flaky broad acted like an egotist to him.

"Hello," Butch said, somewhat stressing the word. He stuffed the rag back in his hip pocket, then stood with his hands on his hips. He now looked obviously annoyed and Sylvia became somewhat surprised, not getting the reaction from this ruggedly attractive man she always got from other men. So she turned on the charm even more.

"I'm Pops Griffiths' niece," she said, "I understand the town is holding a memorial for my uncle?"

"On the high school football field," said Butch, with just a touch of displeasure in his voice. He started to turn away but Sylvia's voice stopped him.

"Where is that?" she asked quickly, not wanting this very appealing man to leave her without succumbing to her charms.

Butch sighed, bored already with this whole situation.

"Take this street all the way down to the second intersection, turn right, go on up to the next intersection, turn left and the road will turn into dirt but just keep following it. The high school is half a mile down."

"Turn right at the next intersection, then go left at the second one?" said Sylvia, in forced confusion. Butch's eyes narrowed, really getting ticked off now. Either this broad was really that dumb or she was making a play for him, but in either case, Butch couldn't stand it.

"No. Second intersection, turn right. Next intersection, turn left," he repeated, somewhat between clenched teeth. Sylvia shook her head in distress.

"Oh, I'm terrible with directions. Would you come with me and show me the way?"

"Lady, I don't have *time*," snapped Butch, becoming out and out angry now.

"But I happen to be having trouble with my car too," said Sylvia, unruffled by Butch's anger. "It's making a horrible rattling sound when I go over thirty. Won't you come to take a listen to that too?"

Butch was really boiling now, having completely seen through her ruse. But the longer he saw the Porsche the more it interested him. If there happened to really be something wrong with the car, he'd have only himself to blame for not looking into it, and he'd always wanted to get inside a really fine automobile like a Porsche. As he realized this, his anger dissipated. And Sylvia, who was a woman ever alert to a man's reactions and moods, sensed that right away, only she mistakenly attributed the cooling of Butch's anger to her charms, not her car's.

"You will want to drive it, won't you?" she said, beginning to open the door.

Butch realized she was back on that track of trying to con him into an attraction to her and got annoyed all over again. But still there was this car...

"No. It would be better if you drove, so I could concentrate on listening to the motor."

"Oh. All right." Sylvia shut the door. Not wanting to possibly dirty the fine interior, Butch peeled off his greasy uniform and tossed it onto the nearest gas pump, under Sylvia's approving gaze. He suddenly had a strange and degrading feeling like he was stripping for this woman, even though all he did was reveal his jeans and cotton work shirt to her. But he felt violated and cheap and his dislike for this woman increased to out and out hatred for her at making him feel this way. He walked around the car and got in on the passenger side without even one glance at Sylvia. But Sylvia watched his every move as he settled in and she smiled superficially charmingly. Then her expression became one of superficial surprise.

"Oh by the way, what's your name?" she asked.

"Butch Przybylski," he replied. He had wondered when she was going to get around to asking him his name. While Sylvia changed gears Butch leaned into the corner between the seat and the door so he was as far away from Sylvia as he could get, and rested one arm over the top of his seat and the other on the top of the door. "And not only am I a mechanic, I'm the town's resident ax murderer, too.'

He grinned wickedly, mocking her, while Sylvia turned her head to look at him in genuine surprise now. There was just the slight sign of nervousness in Sylvia's expression now as she released the clutch and drove the car off.

The mood was now solemn and the congestion at the football field and the parking lot next it was even worse than when the town gathered for a football game, as the time approached for Pops' and Jennie's memorial. It seemed absolutely everybody was coming out for it. Cars blocked other cars and held up the flow of traffic. Dust was kicked up by the stopping and starting of each car, so a gigantic cloud of it hung over the area. Amidst it all Jane valiantly directed the traffic into some kind of order so Galen in the parking lot could direct it into the spaces.

The dust coated her uniform and clung to her mouth. Her nose was really beginning to feel the effect of Steve's slugging it yesterday, and it hurt Jane just to breath through it. It also felt ten times as big despite the ice pack she had put on it last night. The temperature rose to an Indian Summer warm, and perspiration began to drip down Jane's face and back. She could feel her shirt stick to her back and under her arms where she perspired. There was no way she could stop and take her jacket off, as the cars were coming at her one after another with no space in-between. She also felt sore all over from her run-in with Steve, and her arms were especially weary from having had to wave them constantly giving directions to the cars. Jane began to think the doctor had been wrong yesterday when he said she would be able to go to work today. She didn't feel like being here. She didn't want to be here. She felt thoroughly dirty and tired and upset, so much so she found herself agreeing with Butch that this memorial for Pops was a bucket of crap.

The only slight reprieve from her bad mood was when Tim arrived to cover the memorial. He waved at her and smiled as he drove up and she was moved to smile back too. But then she urgently directed him towards the parking lot as she had done to every other car that went by. And his blue Pontiac disappeared into the crowd of cars in the parking lot.

She waved on in the next car, when suddenly in the corner of her eye she spotted a bright red foreign car, a convertible, leave the lineup of other cars and drive up the driveway in the wrong direction. She stared at it curiously, and angrily at the blatant disregard it showed for order and the plainly stated instruction not to enter here, then raised her eyebrows at the sight of the car's gorgeous driver. Feminine intuition told her this must be

Pops' niece Sylvia Griffiths, the fashion plate from Chicago. But her heart caught in her throat when she caught a glimpse of who sat in the passenger seat.

The car in front of her honked her back to her job at hand, but she kept glancing quickly and panicky back towards the red convertible. From the quick looks she could get she saw the driver stop in the driveway, and several of the town council members and the mayor soon gather next to the car. Then she had to look away several seconds, and when she looked back she saw that it was indeed, unmistakably, her Butch with Sylvia, standing behind her while she was chatting with the mayor. The bottom dropped out from under Jane's emotions at this positive realization, and the ensuing whirlwind of devastation and excruciating agony kept her distracted from the annoyance and disgust that was plainly on Butch's face even at the great distance that separated them. All Jane saw through her blur of confusion and pain was that Butch was with another woman, a woman completely the opposite of herself.

But the time Jane joined the crowd in the football field bleachers, the memorial was well underway and the mayor well into his eulogy for Pops, with frequent mention of Jennie in it now as well. She stood a good half a football field away from the small stage and podium he school usually used to crown the homecoming queen, and saw over the crowd's heads Sylvia sitting next to some of the city council members near the edge of the low platform. And next to her on the field stood Butch. Again, Jane was too upset to notice the disgusted, bored look on his face, and had only the presence of mind to fight back the tears that were welling up in her eyes. Nor did she see Tim sitting at the bottom of the bleachers, taking notes of the memorial. He noticed too who was standing next to the beautiful blonde on the platform. After a few minutes Tim began to scan the crowd around him, and spotted Jane at the top. He saw the expression on her face, and he looked pained, yet at the same time, hope sprang into his eyes. The mayor finished speaking, then each city council member spoke, then finally the mayor stood and announced to the gathering Sylvia

Griffiths would like to say a few words regarding her dear uncle. The crowd gave a polite, respectful round of warm applause, and Sylvia stood up. But she did not come forward for a brief second, and then suddenly grasped her hand to her head and fell back, right into Butch, who in a reflect action grabbed her and held her in his arms.

The crowd erupted at this and Jane lost sight of what was happening at the podium. She heard the voice of the mayor say Miss Griffiths was all right, that she had merely fainted under the strain of the occasion, and that the memorial was over and everyone could leave. At the signal Jane knew she had to get back to the driveway and direct the traffic out now. She managed to get to her former position and began directing the traffic back out, pulling on all her professionalism to do so. The traffic was jammed even worse getting out, as everyone was impatient to get back to their normal routine and own lives, and the honking horns and occasional angry shouts increased in number. All this helped Jane, though, to keep her mind on her task at hand and not think about what she had seen with Butch. Still, in the back of her mind she looked to see Butch in the mass exodus, but she never saw him. And when the traffic had cleared and Jane could look around for herself, there was no sign of Butch, or the red convertible, or Sylvia Griffiths.

On her way to Pops' store Jane drove by the Przybylski Garage. There was no sign of Butch but Andy was out front pumping some gas for a customer, and waved happily at her when he recognized her in the patrol car. Jane waved back even though her heart was breaking. The idea crossed her mind to stop in, but she told herself she was on duty and it would be wrong to take time from the taxpayers for a personal matter. She made one final wave at Andy and drove on.

Nothing had been changed, moved, or touched around Pops' store since the previous Friday morning. The yellow police line still surrounded the building, albeit sagging a little, and bobbing up and down in the slight breeze that had kicked up. The breeze was chilly as Jane parked the patrol car out front and got out, causing her to shiver a little, cooling her off and then some from her previous state of overheated at the memorial. The chill was not the pleasant, autumn one of the past Indian Summer days, but bitter in a pre-winter way. Jane zipped up her jacket, then headed back around Pops' store.

It was not Pops' store she was interested in inspecting, but the pathway between it and the Dowagiac. The fallen, brightly hued leaves that layered the pathway rustled between her boots as she walked slowly down it, scanning it and the area around it. When she arrived at the river's edge it was fifteen minutes later, so carefully was her examining of the usually two or three minute walk. The Dowagiac's current was swift as Jane walked up to the edge and scanned the area around her feet. The forest came right up to the bank of the river here, and several large boulders lined the bank inside the river. Jane stood for a moment after examining the ground around her. Then she looked backwards, turned her head back around to the river, and stretched herself out a little towards it. As she did, she glanced to her right, in the direction of the current, and saw it. What she had hoped to find in this long-shot search, that tangible piece of evidence that would enable her to tell the world what had happened to Jennie O'Brien, wedged between two of the large boulders.

A half an hour later Jane and Ralph arrived at their mutual destination in their patrol cars and parked. Ralph followed Jane up the walk, a serious yet curious look on his face. Jane had come into the Sheriff's office with her evidence, and asked Ralph to then come with her. Ralph was not sure what this evidence proved, as Jane declined to tell him here, asking instead to be allowed to wait and explain later, when everything word be cleared up.

Jane rang the doorbell and the door opened, and behind the screen door stood Mrs. Ballard. She was dressed in a black dress and still had on her small black hat.

"Mrs. Ballard, I want to speak to your son," said Jane.

"You can't. He's had a terrible shock, hearing what happened to Jennie. Steve can't talk to anyone."

"He'll have to talk to me. About this."

Jane brought her left hand forward from behind her and showed Mrs. Ballard what was in it. Mrs. Ballard's eyes widened in surprise.

"What! That's Steve's sweater! The one that's been missing!" she exclaimed.

Jane and Ralph were sitting again in the Ballard living room when Mrs. Ballard called upstairs to Steve to please come down. Heavy footsteps were heard coming down the stairs and then Steve appeared. He stopped on the bottom step when he saw Jane and Ralph.

"Steve, the deputy has something to show you," said Mrs. Ballard.

"Steve." Jane stood up and held the sweater out towards him. It was still slightly damp despite the heavy wringing Jane gave it. "Is this sweater yours?"

Steve stood looking at it, panic growing in his eyes. Mrs. Ballard was as curious about Jane having the sweater as Ralph, only she did not care for the confrontational attitude Jane was taking with Steve about it.

"Where did you find that, Deputy?" she asked, slightly sharp.

"On the bank of the Dowagiac. Behind Pops Griffiths' general store."

"In the river?" said Mrs. Ballard, surprised. She looked at her son. "How did your good sweater get in the river behind the Griffiths' store?"

"Yes Steve. How did it get there?" asked Jane.

Steve was growing even more panicky as the seconds went by, but he still held on to a little self-control.

"I don't know," he said.

Mrs. Ballard looked shocked at her son's answer. Ralph continued to look solemn, as slowly things began to come together in his mind, at least about the sweater and its connection to Pops Griffiths. Jane's expression did not change as she unfolded the sweater and held the front of it towards Steve.

"I guess you don't know how this blood got on it either," she said.

Mrs. Ballard and Ralph stared at the sweater flat in Jane's hands in surprise. Ralph was surprised because Jane had not shown him this aspect of the sweater when she had come in to the Sheriff's office. The large spots were a little faded, as the river water had washed some of it out of the weave, but they were undeniably made of blood.

"And I'm further guessing you don't know whose blood this is, either," said Jane.

Mrs. Ballard finally found her voice.

"Deputy, just what are you insinuating about my son!" she said, getting angry.

Jane looked at Steve.

"Should I tell her, Steve? Or do you want to tell her" she asked.

Steve was completely quivering with panic now, yet remained silent. Jane could see slight twitches around his mouth and from his lips, as if only a hair's breadth away from telling all. So Jane then pressed on harder on him.

"Do you want me to tell her it's Pops Griffiths' blood?" said Jane.

"Pops Griffiths!" repeated Mrs. Ballard, "Deputy, are you accusing my son of…"

"Yes Mom! That's what she's saying!"

Steve finally broke down and anguish filled his face. He slumped down onto the chair behind him.

"Last Friday night. Jennie and I didn't go to Pebble Creek. We went to Pops' store instead."

"Why, Steve?" asked Mrs. Ballard.

Tears began to stream down Steve's face, yet he retained that small amount of control he had earlier and continued on.

"SO…so…Pops could take care of her," he said.

"Take care of her? Take care of what?" asked Mrs. Ballard.

Steve swallowed heavily and wiped his face with his hands, though tears continued to pour down his face.

"Jennie…was…was gonna have a baby," he said.

Ralph now became as shocked as Mrs. Ballard, this a whole new angle to him. Jane however remained passive and watched Steve carefully.

"She…we…got into trouble. Last month, we…were together, at her place."

Then two weeks ago Jennie comes and tells me she's late, she hasn't had her period, and she's pretty sure she's pregnant. We didn't know what to do, till she told her friend Mary Jo about it, and she said she could arrange everything to take care of it."

"What did she arrange Steve?" asked Ralph, totally stunned.

"She arranged it with Pops Griffiths, to take care of it. To give her an abortion."

"Pops? Give her an abortion?" said Mrs. Ballard breathlessly. She looked as if she had been punched in the chest with a sledgehammer.

"He'd...done it for her, Mary Jo, and a couple other girls at school. This wasn't supposed to happen! Everything was supposed to go fine, just like all those other girls! Jennie wasn't supposed to get hurt!"

"But she did get hurt, didn't she, Steve?" said Jane, quietly and solemnly.

"Yes!" sobbed Steve, "I was waiting in the kitchen, and all of a sudden I hear Jennie screaming and crying and their struggling, and I run in the bathroom and there's Jennie sitting on the toilet, and Pops with this big knife all covered in blood in his hand and trying to make Jennie sit still. And there was blood all over! All over Jennie, and she didn't have anything on below her waist, and on Pops, and all over the toilet and the floor around it..." Steve's voice caught in his throat and he looked deadly sick. "All I remember is running in there, and grabbing the knife in Pops' hand, and then the next thing I knew I was standing over Pops and he had that knife in his chest and there was more blood everywhere. I looked at him a long time, trying to see if he was breathing. But then I remember Jennie, and when I looked at her..." Steve's face twisted into it's most anguished expression now. "I knew she was dead. I didn't have to look at her much..."

Mrs. Ballard, with tears streaming down her face now, knelt next to her son and held him. Ralph, now as devastated in his own way, glanced away from the mother and son. Only Jane continued to look passive.

"Then what happened Steve?" she said softly but firmly.

"I didn't know what I should do. I couldn't think. The only thing I could think of to do was do something about Jennie. So I went to the bedroom and took the bedspread and wrapped her up in it, with her clothes, and I carried her out and I..." Steve sobbed through his last words. "...threw her in the river."

Steve broke down completely and Mrs. Ballard gathered him closer in her arms. Ralph rubbed his face and squirmed in his place, now so overwhelmed at what he heard he could barely stand it. Jane now finally looked affected as she saw Steve would not be able to say more.

"And when you noticed your sweater covered in blood, you tossed that in there too," she said quietly, "Only not quite far enough."

Steve didn't have to nod, but the three of them knew that was his last action in the horrible drama that had taken place that death-filled night.

***

Steve was arrested and taken to the Sheriff's office, where he was fingerprinted, photographed and placed in the Grangeville jail to await his arraignment. The lawyer Mrs. Ballard called was due in a half hour to consult with his client. Ralph shut the office door to the jail area, shaking his head. Clark had been there when Jane and Ralph had brought Steve in, and was just getting over his stunned speechlessness from being told why Steve Ballard came in hand cuffs.

"My God. My God," said Ralph. He hung the jail keys up and shook his head yet again in disbelief. "How can anything like this happen here in Grangeville?"

"No place is immune to horrid acts, Sheriff," said Jane.

Ralph looked at her carefully, and with more respect that anytime before.

"You knew this was what happened all along, didn't you, Deputy. From the beginning, at the discovery of Pops' body, you knew what had happened. How did you know? What did you see in all that blood that told you?" he asked.

"It wasn't the sight of blood, Sheriff," said Jane, "It was something I smelled."

Both Clark and Ralph looked puzzled.

"Smelled?" asked Clark.

"Yes. The toilet in Pops' bathroom. The blood in the toilet had an odor. A menstrual odor."

Clark and Ralph flushed completely red with embarrassment, overwhelming their shock at the situation. A small part of Jane was amused at their reaction, but she kept her demeanor solemn and professional.

"The forensic analysis of the blood will show it was menstrual. But the odor was right there. For anyone who is familiar with it." Jane now made a half smile. "Which would only be a female. And I am female. As we all here know."

Ralph and Clark continued to be embarrassed, but now startled, and Jane was moved to continue on with her explanation that had been bottled up inside her for so long.

"But it was the attitude you just expressed, Sheriff, that how could anything like illegal abortions happen in Grangeville, which kept me from coming to you with this, without some kind of concrete evidence," she continued, "I had all this circumstantial evidence: the odor, Jennie missing and no indication of her a runaway or kidnapped, her blood type the same as the other found at the scene. And Pops found dead in his bathroom, and not really the saint everyone thought." This she remembered came from Butch, and she winced inwardly at the thought of him. "His bedspread missing and then found in the Dowagiac." Another inward wince at remembering who had done the finding. "I had all this, but if I came to you and said Pops was an abortionist and blotched an abortion on Jennie, you still wouldn't have believed me."

Ralph now began to feel a little annoyed at Jane for not thinking he could be professional and open-minded enough to hear her theory, yet he knew she was right, he couldn't have believed her, and that made him even more annoyed. And he didn't like it either that only Jane could immediately have noticed that important clue of the odor that linked Pops' and Jennie's cases. But with this newly found respect for Jane, he couldn't direct that emotion towards her, so he went for another target.

"Well, abortions are wrong, anyway. It's wrong for a girl to have one."
Jane's ire was aroused.

"Easy for you to say Ralph," she stated, almost snapping the words out,
"You'll never be pregnant."

"I still know what's right and wrong," said Ralph, letting the fact Jane
called him by his first name pass, as if it were the most natural thing in the
world for her to do now.

"Only for women. Maybe we women ought to return the favor.
Make a decision that only affects you men. Decide when you should
have a vasectomy."

Ralph flushed red at that. But it galvanized Clark to speak.

"Well, if you women would just learn to keep your legs together till
you're married, you wouldn't need abortions," he said.

Jane now knew she'd better get out of there before she really got mad
and things really escalated. She grabbed her car keys up from her desk, but
she couldn't resist a parting shot.

"We'll learn that when you guys learn to keep your pecker in your
pants," she snapped.

This time Clark flushed red. Jane was almost out the door when Ralph's
voice stopped her.

"Wait a minute," he said firmly and loudly. Jane stopped at the door
and turned around. Suddenly, for the first time in her career in the
Grangeville Sheriff's Department, Jane sensed a conciliatory feeling in the
air, a desire to compromise, work things out, to accept her, and all that she
represented and added to the department. Ralph lost his embarrassed
look, and once again he wore an expression of respect on his face for Jane.

"This isn't something for us in this department to decide. We each have
our own opinion. What we need to do is just respect that."

"That's all that's ever needed, Sheriff," said Jane.

Ralph looked at Clark, and he nodded too.

"Fine. Then let's get back to work," said Ralph.

He went into his office and shut the door. Clark went to his desk. Jane turned back around and went out to finish her shift on patrol.

***

There was a figure standing in his fishing spot and as Butch got closer he saw it was Jane. When he stepped through the brush Jane, who had been looking out to the water, turned slightly away from the river to look at him, her hands in her jacket pockets, the jacket zipped all the way up against the chill that now permeated the air.

It was as if Indian Summer had suddenly ended right then, that day, that afternoon just as Jane's shift ended. The sky was overcast with heavy gray clouds and a definite wintry chill hung in the air. The trees, though still full of leaves, had the leaves hanging from them like so many colorful yet drab wet socks. That fine warm glow of the last gasp of summer warmth had been extinguished like a candle being snuffed out.

Jane looked at Butch a moment with a look in her eyes like something had been extinguished in her, then to Butch's surprise she turned away from him.

"Janie," he said, "I've been looking for you all afternoon."

"Why?" she asked, surprising Butch further.

"Why? Because I haven't seen you since you got off work. I went home and you weren't there and you weren't at your apartment. I checked Uncle Nunzio's and I even went to the Sheriff's office." Butch's tone went serious "They told me you cracked the case about Pops' murder and the O'Brien girl's disappearance." Butch smiled. "I'm so proud of you," he added, then he looked serious again, "I was also worried about not finding you. Especially after that odd conversation with Tim Usher."

"Odd?" asked Jane, that word bringing up the memory of his odd kiss yesterday.

"Yeah. I ran into him a little while ago. I don't know what that guy was getting at, but I didn't like it. He asked me some really weird questions,

like, what did I think of Sylvia Griffiths and did I like her and was I happy
to meet her and did I like escorting her to the memorial. Stuff like that."

At the mention of Sylvia Griffiths Jane bowed her head and winced, visibly this time. This action finally exasperated Butch and he became annoyed.
He went over to her and pulled her around to him by her left arm.

"What is the matter with you?" he asked, "You're acting like you've lost
your best friend."

"Haven't I?" Jane asked, not raising her head.

Butch was stunned but also more annoyed at being further shoved in
the dark.

"What are you talking about?" he demanded.

"Haven't I lost *you*? To Sylvia Griffiths?" she said in a small voice.

Butch was now stunned speechless while Jane turned away from him
again. He stared at her a few moments till he finally recovered his voice.

"No. You haven't lost me to Sylvia Griffiths," he said firmly, "What in
the world gave you that idea?"

Jane's expression became painful and for the first time since he'd known
her, Butch saw tears appear in her eyes.

"You went with her to her uncle's memorial, didn't you? I saw you
together, I saw you two arrive," she said, "You were with her during the
service. You caught her when she fainted."

"She didn't really faint. That broad did that for effect," said Butch. Then
he realized Jane was taking this seriously. "Janie, I didn't go with her to
Pops' memorial. She couldn't comprehend how to get there, the dunce, and
claimed there was something wrong with her car, so she asked me to ride
along to listen to the engine too. Then when I wanted to stay in the car till
the memorial was over she said she couldn't remember how the mayor told
her to get from where she parked to the football field. So I had to take her
there. I hung around because I did hear something odd with the engine
and wanted to get a look at it. It was a Porsche, you know." Butch grinned,
then became serious again. "Hell, you couldn't have guessed this woman
had "fainted" only about an hour before by the way she ranted and raved at

me for taking so much time fixing her engine." Butch's tone lightened a little. "I will admit I tinkered around a little more than necessary, but who knows when I'll get my hands on a Porsche engine again?" Butch's tone then became slightly smug. "Seems Miss Griffiths couldn't wait to get out of town when no one seemed concerned about her anymore after she "came to" and Dr. Ekert declared nothing was wrong and she was all right. The only one who still had any interest in her staying was Galen, but he was shaking in his boots so bad when he met her, and then the shrew she was at the garage made him take off like a bat out of hell." Butch smiled, amused at the memory. "That's why you saw me with Sylvia Griffiths, Janie. I didn't have nor do I have any interest in her."

But Jane's expression still did not change, and Butch looked puzzled.

"Janie, don't you believe me?" he asked.

Jane's expression became more painful and tears now actually fell down her cheeks.

"Butch, she's so…so…feminine," she choked out.

"Feminine?" Butch repeated, more puzzled.

"She's beautiful, and sophisticated and rich and glamorous, and she dresses and acts so womanly," said Jane quickly, "How can you not be attracted to her instead of me? You have to be. She's what men like and want. Not me."

Jane wiped her eyes but the tears kept coming and kept her cheeks wet. Butch stood watching her, now expressionless.

"I thought I had put all that kind of thinking behind me, but today, when I saw her with you, and I love you so much Butch, it came all crashing back on me." Jane took a long ragged breath. "Sylvia's like a…a croissant, Butch," she said, a slight flippant edge to her tone,

"All light and delicate and rich and special. I'm…I'm like a regular old average piece of white bread. Why would a man want a slice of that when he could have something better?"

Jane finally turned her head towards Butch and looked up at him, but not directly, her lids shaded her eyes. She sniffed several times and wiped her eyes. Butch said nothing while Jane slowly stopped crying. When she did he finally spoke.

"'Something better,'" he repeated flatly, "What makes you think a flaky croissant is better than a good solid slice of white bread?"

Jane was moved with the hope Butch's words evoked in her. She shifted slightly and shrugged her shoulders and shook her head tentatively.

"What makes you think I'd want someone superficial and shallow over someone solid and substantial? I thought you knew me better than that, Jane Marie Fleming."

Butch put his fingers under Jane's chin and raised her face so they looked at each other eye to eye.

"I thought it was pretty much settled that I love you, Janie. I'm pretty sure I've said it enough times. But I'll say it again. I love you."

Butch suddenly embraced Jane tightly and kissed her hard. Jane was so surprised, and overwhelmed at Butch's intensity, her breath was taken away.

"Oh Butch," she whispered, after taking a deep breath when they released the kiss, her voice heavy with happiness. All uncertainty was gone from her now. Butch still held her tightly, slightly pulling her up on her toes to keep her mouth to mouth with him.

"I want you to remember this. And that you are the only woman for me. I don't want some flaky shell of a croissant. I want a good solid slice of white bread I can sink my teeth into." Butch grinned slyly, baring his teeth.

"Oh Butch," repeated Jane, starting to cry again, but now for happiness.

"And to make sure you always remember." Butch paused, his smile fading and a devil-may-care but totally serious look came on his face. "I want you to marry me."

"Oh Butch," said Jane, overwhelmed. Butch scowled slightly.

"What's the matter with you? You lost your vocabulary completely except for 'Oh Butch?'" he said. Jane giggled over her tears and shook her head.

"No. I haven't."

Butch then glared at her inquisitively.

"Then will you give me an answer? Will you make an honest man out of me? Will you marry me?"

"Yes. Yes, I'll marry you. Michael," she said. Butch's eyes widened in surprise at her use of his real name.

"Oh. So I guess you're sincere about that answer," he said.

Jane tilted her head a little farther back to look Butch right in the eye, strongly, decisively and confidently.

"You're damned right I am," she said.

Butch grinned approvingly, and they kissed. Then Butch reached up and took hold of her head with his thumbs by her temples. Jane shut her eyes and waited for Butch to kiss them. But to her surprise, she felt him place his nose in the corner of her right eye and slowly draw it across the lid. Then he did it on her left one. When he finished Jane opened her eyes and looked at him in surprise.

"You can't do it for me for a while," he said, touching her still tender nose with the tip of his first finger gently, "So it's time I started doing it for you."

***

The church bells began to peal briskly in the bright clear May air when the newlywed Mr. and Mrs. Michael "Butch" Przybylski emerged in the church doorway. Butch looked devilishly handsome in his black tuxedo with the black velvet vest and bow tie. Jane lacked nothing on Sylvia Griffiths in beauty in her simple but elegant long white wedding gown. There were a few whispers on how Jane could wear white, but the happiness and relief felt at she and Butch finally tying the knot drowned out any criticisms. Her veil crowned her head and fell back all the way to the floor, and them some. The sunshine hit them both when they stepped out onto the top church step, making Jane's dress dazzle and Butch's tuxedo shine. The crowd before them began to cheer and throw rice.

No invitations had been mailed, Butch sent out by word of mouth that anybody in Grangeville who wanted to come to his and Jane's wedding were welcome to come, and it appeared anyone who heard the word had come. There were both sets of parents: Jane's folks from Detroit and Butch's from Fort Wayne, Indiana; Jane's older brother and younger sister, who was maid of honor; Butch's two sisters who were bridesmaids; Butch's cousin Joe and his uncle, Principal Henry Ross. Pete, and Andy, Sy and Wil, who were best man and ushers, respectively; Lonnie Sargent and the rest of the Przybylski Pit Bulls. Ralph, Galen, Clark and the rest the Sheriff's deputies were there, all quite surprised to see Jane look so lovely and in a dress. Gracie and her family were there, Gracie taking off the day from Ma's Restaurant to be there, declaring she would quit if she couldn't be at her favorite customers' wedding. George and Edna Robbins were there, as well as Alice French, who out beamed even Jane's mother at seeing Jane now a married woman. There was Uncle Nunzio himself, Ray McKinney, who was catering the reception in the Pebble Creek Pavilion, for free as his wedding present; Randy Monaghan and Walter Terry, whose devotion to Jane had caught and grown after their little escapade in the school; Lloyd Bunker, the voice of the Przybylski Pit Bulls; Dr. Ekert was there with his wife and three children; Coach Warneke and the whole Grangeville High football team; Stanley Ross and Wendall Polen, long having made up after their traffic accident when each of their insurance companies paid for their damages, after their small deductibles; and Jane's landlord, Reese Butterworth, who stated he was sorry he was losing such a quiet and good tenant for the apartment above his drugstore. Then there were all the others of the population of Grangeville, so many that they filled the pews in the church, lined the walls and overflowed outside.

But not everyone down to the last person attended the Fleming – Przybylski wedding. The Ballards stayed away, still getting their lives together after the tragedy regarding Steve. Steve had been convicted of a reduced charge of manslaughter that his lawyer plea bargained down to in return for a guilty plea, thus avoiding a long and painful and ugly trial. He was now serving time in a juvenile prison farm near Grand Rapids, close enough for his parents to visit him often. And it appeared Steve would one day be released; he was not charged as an adult, and he was eligible for parole and a model prisoner.

The O'Briens did not attend, they had been all set to move from Grangeville in shame, but their many friends and the other townspeople convinced them not to, for it meant also Bill O'Brien selling his hardware store that had been in his family for three generations. So they stayed, but kept mostly to themselves for several months, and only now were getting their lives back to normal, like the Ballards.

Nor did Tim Usher attend the wedding. He sold the Chronicle in February after having it up for sale since November, and moved to Chicago. When asked why he was selling the paper, he said the coverage of Pops' murder and Jennie's death from an illegal abortion had made him realize he wasn't ready to give up big stories like that; his retirement from the fast lane was premature. So he sold the Chronicle to Ray McKinney's nephew, a graduate from MSU with a journalism degree, and joined the Sun-Times. Jane was sad to see him go, as sad as Tim got when Jane came in to the place her engagement announcement in the paper, though he masked it carefully.

The final forensic results confirmed all of the circumstances Jane suspected: some threads from the bedspread found in the Dowagiac matched those in Pops' bedroom, some of the blood in the bathroom was menstrual blood, Steve's fingerprints matched those on the knife that killed Pops, Jennie's complete autopsy showed she had had a botched abortion. When the whole story came out, more girls came forward to report they had had abortions by Pops too, seventeen girls in all, even some in junior high.

Sylvia Griffiths tried to sell her uncle's store, though not personally. She contacted the Grangeville Real Estate Office from Chicago and had them list the business for sale, but not surprisingly, there were not too many offers from anyone in town. Finally the Grangeville Real Estate Office bought the place itself, and remodeled it for a larger office, as the real estate company was expanding. A farmer outside of Grangeville had sold his farm to a developer, and Grangeville was getting a brand new expensive subdivision that would make the homes on Southview Street look shabby, and a large influx of new people. Already the first few new homes were up and new people had moved in.

And the previous January, a decision had been made that Grangeville now had a reason to have an interest in. The Supreme Court of the United States ruled abortions were legal in a case called Roe vs. Wade. When Jane heard of the decision, she let out an inner sigh of relief that now there would be no more Jennie O'Briens in Grangeville, or anywhere else in the country for that matter.

So big things were happening to and in Grangeville, and the May wedding of Butch and Jane was one of those things. They announced their engagement on Halloween, which was Butch's idea. They placed an announcement in the Grangeville Chronicle, including a picture of both Jane and Butch in it, the addition of Butch a shock to the society arbitrators of Grangeville. Then the date was set for May, and Alice French held a bridal shower for Jane in April. While everyone seemed pleased that Butch and Jane were getting married, there was an undercurrent of disappointment that everyone's favorite illicit couple would soon be just an regular old married one and the spice they enlivened Grangeville with soon would be gone too.

But none of that feeling was evident when Jane appeared in the doorway of the church on her father's arm. The congregation rose at the sight of them and it watched Jane and Richard Fleming walked down the aisle. But while all eyes were on Jane and her father, all Jane saw from the moment she appeared in the doorway till she reached the end was Butch standing there smiling that devil-may-care grin of his and beaming with confidence. His confidence dissolved the small case of nerves Jane had, and they proceeded through the ceremony calmly and assuredly. There was a quiet little ripple of surprise when the minister announced Jane and Butch had written their own vows, and the congregation then realized the team of Butch and Jane would not stop shaking them up just because they were getting married. After their vows, in which they promised to recognize each other as individuals and help each other to develop to the fullest and to share their lives with each other, they exchanged rings, Pete nervously handing the minister both golden orbs. The minister pronounced them husband and wife, and Mr. Przybylski planted a firm kiss on the Mrs. Przybylski who was not his mother.

Pete drove the newlyweds to the Pebble Creek Pavilion in Butch's Mustang, decorated with steamers and balloons and the big sign in the back declaring the couple just married. He lead the procession of cars carrying the wedding guests and the reception was soon in full swing under the huge pavilion. Toast after toast was made to the newlyweds, Pete starting them off with the best man toast. Even Ralph made a toast, declaring Jane a good deputy and may she have a good marriage. Jane was struck speechless at this.

After the fine meal Ray had set out it was time to cut the cake. The baker at the Grangeville Heavenly Home-Baked Bakery wheeled out a quite large and very elaborately decorated five-tiered cake to the loud exclamations of the guests. They expected some hi-jinks from Butch and Jane with the sharing of the first piece, but instead they both did it quite solemnly and seriously, deciding beforehand not to ridicule what this action represented. But after they had both fed each other a piece, Butch grabbed Jane's hand and ate the frosting that had gotten on her fingers to Jane's amusement.

As the afternoon stretched into evening there was only one more thing for them to do before taking off to start their honeymoon. Butch removed Jane's garter to accompanying proper music, and Jane stood to throw her bouquet. All the single women gathered behind her to catch it, but just as Jane threw it over her head, a strong gust of wind caught it and it went sailing off to the side. The green and white bouquet landed in the hands of Walter Terry standing next to the edge of the pavilion.

There was some discussion as to what to do next. Butch was in favor of Wil, who had caught the garter, putting it on Walter, much to Wil's disappointment and Walter's disgust. But finally it was decided Walter would toss the bouquet himself to the group of single women. He did, and Amanda McKinney, Ray's daughter, caught it. Wil gave no resistance to putting it up pretty nineteen-year-old Amanda's leg. Though he did it under the watchful eye of Uncle Nunzio.

Jane and Butch remained a few minutes longer at the reception, saying goodbye to their parents and siblings. Then, while the reception was going full swing with the music and dancing and continued eating and drinking, the new Mr. and Mrs. Przybylski slipped away in their decorated Mustang.

***

The hot pink neon lights of the LaPierre were on and blazing when Butch and Jane pulled up close to midnight. Butch pulled into their regular spot and parked. He got out and then helped Jane hold her wedding dress so she could get out too.

The manager of the LaPierre looked up when Jane and Butch came in, dressed in their wedding splendor. There was a fleeting look of recognition on his face at the sight of Butch, but it was soon replaced with surprise at what he was wearing and a woman dressed as a bride with him.

"Good evening, Mr. Przybylski," said the manager. Butch noticed the surprised look on the man's face.

"You have my reservation ready for me?" Butch asked.

"Your usual room, Mr. Przybylski," said the manager. He slid the registration book towards Butch. "Would you sign here please?"

Butch took the pen from the man and signed. The manager read the signature.

"'Mr. and Mrs. Michael Przybylski'?" he read, now looking puzzled.

"Let me explain. Mr. And Mrs. *Butch* Przybylski just made legal. We're on our way to Mackinac Island for our honeymoon."

"I see," said the manager, now looking pleased. He smiled as Jane, who had been standing there, smiled herself. Suddenly Butch put down the pen and picked Jane up in his arms while the manager removed the keys to the unit from the board beside him.

"Your keys, Mrs. Przybylski," said the manager, turning back to him and surprised now to find Butch holding his bride in his arms.

"Thank you," said Jane, "I'll take them." And she did.

"Make sure we're not disturbed," said Butch, as he started to walk out of the office carrying Jane. The manager watched as Jane opened the door and they went through it, and then watched them through the windows reach their usual room, where Jane unlocked the door and Butch and she disappeared into it.

"As usual, Mr. Przybylski," he said.

The End